love

among

the walnuts

love among the walnuts

jean ferris

Harcourt Brace & Company

San Diego   New York   London

Library of Congress Cataloging-in-Publication Data
Ferris, Jean, 1939–
Love among the walnuts/Jean Ferris.
p. cm.
Summary: Born and raised in isolation in a wealthy,
eccentric family, Sandy is shocked when he, his parents,
and their servants become victims of a vicious plot
by his greedy uncles to incapacitate them and take their money.
ISBN 0-15-201590-6
[1. Crime—Fiction. 2. Wealth—Fiction. 3. Uncles—Fiction.]
I. Title.
PZ7.F4174Lr 1998
[Fic]—dc21   97-50291

Text set in Sabon
Designed by Camilla Filancia

C E F D B
Printed in the United States of America

To the memory of

JACKIE DEWEY EVERINGHAM

who named this book

and who knew plenty about love

part one

CHAPTER

1

Once upon a time there was a very wealthy young man named Horatio Alger Huntington-Ackerman. When he was a little boy he liked the fact that his initials spelled HAHA, because he found that in spite of some problems with his family, there was a lot to laugh about. But as he grew up and made his vast fortune and dealt with the world, it seemed that there were fewer and fewer things to feel HAHA about.

Two of the things that were making his enjoyment of life less than it had been were his brothers, Bartholemew Algernon Huntington (who hadn't gotten along with his father and so didn't use the Ackerman) and Bernard Aloysius Ackerman (who hadn't gotten along with his mother and so didn't use the Huntington). Interestingly, both the brothers' initials made the same sound, though spelled differently.

Bart and Bernie were younger than Horatio, and when they were children they had all gotten along well. Horatio was the big brother and so tried to be a good example for his younger siblings. But when they grew up, Bart and Bernie were unable to duplicate Horatio's splendid successes, and they became jealous and mean-spirited. Horatio enjoyed their company less and less, until one day, he discovered he didn't enjoy it at all.

Although Horatio lived in an elegant town house in the choicest midtown location near his office buildings, stockbrokers, banks, financial advisers, lawyers, tax accountants, and health club, he gradually came to realize that all these things—considered by many (including Bart and Bernie) to be among the finest life had to offer—were not making him as happy as he had been in his childhood, when he had had none of them.

Furthermore, it upset his digestion to spend all day wearing a three-piece suit and watching other men and women struggle to achieve what he had, sometimes by means of which he couldn't approve. When he tried to tell them that what he had achieved was no guarantee of happiness, they said, "Of course not, we know that." But he could tell by the look in their eyes that they didn't believe him.

There were more and more days when it was difficult for Horatio to leave his elegant town house; more and more days when he put on his maroon silk dressing gown and went into his library instead of going to work. He took down from the tall dark shelves the books from his childhood that had given him such pleasure: *The Wonderful Wizard of Oz*, *Treasure Island*, *Peter Pan*, *The Wind in the Willows*, and The Chronicles of Narnia. He sat in his deep, leather wing chair and read his books and a smile appeared on his lips—a smile that was absent when he was in his office.

Horatio realized, of course, that this was not a healthy thing for him to be doing. He was a young man with a successful business empire that was making him lots of money. He had many acquaintances, which some people regard as the same as having many friends, and invitations to more things than he could possibly attend. He was also quite nice looking and talented at other things besides making money. He could play the guitar, model lifelike animals from clay, and play pool like a professional.

Bentley, his valet, worried about him. He suggested endless games of pool. He bought pounds of clay, which lay untouched in the studio. He brought home new guitar music. He planned parties, trips to art galleries, and excursions to the park and the movies.

Horatio sometimes agreed to go, but he was always glad to get home again, to his library and his old books.

One day Bentley presented Horatio with two tickets to *Social Service,* the hottest new musical in town. Tickets were expensive and almost impossible to get, and Bentley had gone to a lot of trouble to obtain them.

"It's supposed to be the best show in years, Horatio," Bentley said. "Who would you like me to call to go with you?"

"Why don't you use the tickets, Bentley?" Horatio asked. "Take Flossie. I'll even treat you both to dinner any place you want."

"I got these tickets for *you,*" Bentley said. "And you

must use them. You can't keep sitting around here moping and reading in that dark library. You've got to get back out into the world."

"Why?" Horatio asked. "I've got more money than anybody could sensibly want. There's no reason to make any more. The world is an ugly place, full of crime and pollution. Not to mention Bart and Bernie." He shuddered at the thought of them. "I've decided to stay as far away from it as possible."

He hadn't actually decided any such thing, but the minute he said that, he knew it was what he *had* decided to do. "You go," he said to Bentley. "Take Flossie. She'll love it."

Bentley had been engaged to Flossie for eleven years. He loved her dearly and definitely intended to marry her someday, just as soon as he quit being afraid that marriage meant the end of romance.

"No," Bentley said firmly. "These tickets are for you, and you're going to use them if I have to carry you there on my back. If you won't go with anybody else, *I'll* go with you."

Horatio sighed, knowing he would have to go to avoid hurting Bentley's feelings, but dreading the thought of getting all dressed up, being driven through the city traffic in the Daimler, and fighting the crowds at the theater. The trip would be even worse if somebody recognized him. Then a crowd would gather and the people would want to touch him and get his autograph; and strange women would give him their phone numbers. He wished Bentley would leave him alone.

CHAPTER

2

- - - - - - -

The night of the play, Horatio did his best. He got dressed in his tuxedo and his shiny patent leather shoes, and the outfit did make him feel a little better. Shuffling around in his dressing gown was a lonely and gloomy thing to do.

The traffic wasn't too bad, and the Daimler was quiet and comfortable and air-conditioned. People recognized him in the lobby of the theater, but they were polite and respectful for once.

The play was about a wealthy and eccentric woman who was a social crusader. She was so busy she had time only for her work, and she had a fleet of young women to do everything else for her. One chewed her gum for her, one carried her purse for her, one dressed and undressed her, one held the telephone so she could write with both hands while she talked on the phone.

The wealthy woman wanted only beauty around her because she thought ugliness was distracting and interfered with her work. Therefore, all her helpers were gorgeous and wore beautiful things. One of the woman's eccentricities was requiring the young women to wear only white clothing, and white fur coats. (The fur was fake because she didn't want real animals dying for the coats.) The white clothes were made of the finest silks and satins and cottons, lavish with lace and ribbons and ruffles.

The young woman who held the telephone captured Horatio's attention from the beginning of the play. With her glossy brown curls and thick dark eyelashes, she wasn't any more beautiful than any of the others, but her eyes seemed friendly, and the corners of her mouth, even in repose, turned up in a smile. *Only someone with a smile inside herself could look like that,* Horatio thought.

At intermission he searched the program for her name, but since the actresses didn't have speaking parts, they were all lumped together under the heading of HELPERS. Was she Fifi Fernandez? Poodles Pennington? Fleur LaRoche? Mousey Malone?

The minute the curtain closed at the end of the play, he ran backstage, with a bewildered Bentley hurrying behind him. They burst into the dressing room where the actresses were taking off their makeup and changing their clothes. Bentley, enjoying the shrieks and scurrying, was glad he hadn't brought Flossie. Horatio noticed nothing but his beautiful, smiling girl.

She sat at a dressing table, her fingers in a jar of cold cream. Horatio took her hands, not even noticing the cold cream squeezed between his fingers and hers, and said into her surprised face, "Fleur?"

She shook her head and the ends of her smile turned up a little.

"Poodles?" he asked.

She shook her head again and smiled a little more.

"Then it's Fifi?"

Again she shook her head. "Mousey," she said in a small and squeaky voice. "Mousey Malone."

Being treated to the full power of Mousey's smile was like walking into a rainbow. "Mousey Malone," Horatio said, dazed. "What a beautiful name. My name is Ho . . . ah, Homer Smith. Mousey, please have dinner with me. I've something important I must talk to you about."

"Are you an honest man, Homer Smith? An honorable man? A respectful man?" she asked earnestly.

"Oh yes, I am."

"Then I'd love to," she squeaked, gently removing her slippery hands from his. "I'll meet you outside."

Horatio paced in the hall in front of the dressing room. "Bentley, have you ever seen a more beautiful girl? Have you ever seen a more beautiful smile? That girl has the secret for finding joy in life, I know it. Nobody could smile like that if she didn't know where to find joy. I have a feeling she's the answer."

"What's the question?" Bentley asked, pleased, though somewhat startled that his plan to cheer Horatio up had worked even better than he'd hoped.

Horatio ignored him. "I feel better right now than I have in months. I want to marry that girl, Bentley. I *need* to marry her." He stopped pacing and took the lapels of Bentley's tuxedo in his hands. "Do you think she'd have me? I know this is sudden but my business hunches are never wrong; and I don't think this hunch is wrong, either. Do you think she'd be interested?"

Bentley looked at his crumpled lapels. "Maybe. You're young, rich, handsome, honest, unaffected, sincere, and well educated. Though why she'd want to give up a career as a struggling actress who can't get a speaking part in a play, I wouldn't know."

Horatio's hands dropped from Bentley's lapels. "Oh, no. I never thought of that. Her career."

Just then the dressing-room door opened and Mousey came out, wrapped in a fake mink coat. "Here I am," she said with her little voice and big smile.

"Wonderful, Mousey, you look just wonderful," Horatio said, his eyes glazed with admiration. "My car's just outside." Without removing his gaze from Mousey, he said, "Bentley, take us someplace nice and come back in four hours." He held his arm out to Mousey, who solemnly took it. Bentley took his other arm and guided them both out the door.

CHAPTER

3

- - - - - - -

Horatio and Mousey were settled at a corner table in the best restaurant in town, screened from the other diners by a leafy potted tree. The waiter had just poured their first glass of champagne.

Horatio raised his glass. "To your performance. I couldn't take my eyes off you." They sipped. Horatio leaned toward her. "What is the secret of joy?"

Mousey thought for a moment. "Doing what you like best."

"Of course," he said. "How simple. And how true." He hesitated. "And what you like best is acting?"

"I'm never happier than when I'm on a stage," she said, and looked sadly down into her champagne.

"What's wrong?" Horatio asked anxiously.

"This is probably the last play I'll ever be in."

"Why do you say that? Your performance was—" He couldn't think of a word good enough.

"Listen to me," she said. "My *voice*. Why do you think everybody calls me Mousey?"

"Well, can't you take voice lessons? You have such wonderful stage presence. You just need to learn to . . . to project a little," he said tactfully.

"I've tried that. There's something wrong with my voice. I'll never be able to project past the second row. But I love the stage." Tears trembled on her thick lashes.

Horatio took her hand. "What about nonspeaking parts?" he asked tenderly.

"How many of those do you think there are? I'm tired of being a chorus girl and a spear carrier. This is the best part I've had in my whole career, and I'm not likely to find another one like it. I just have to face it. I'm finished." Two iridescent tears slid down her pearly cheeks. Horatio watched in fascination and pain.

"What if you had your own theater, one with only two rows, where you could do anything you want, and you wouldn't have to worry about projecting?"

"What kind of theater has only two rows? Who would come to a theater like that?"

"I would," he said. "It could be a theater in your own house."

"Don't be cruel," she said. "I live in a fourth-floor walk-up with a bathroom down the hall."

"I mean in *our* house."

"What?" Her tears hesitated momentarily.

"*Our* house," Horatio repeated. "Mousey, will you marry me?"

"You told me you were an honest and honorable

and respectful man. I don't think it's very nice of you to make fun of me."

"I only lied to you once, when I told you my name was Homer Smith. Everything else is true, I swear it."

"Homer Smith, who *are* you?"

He took a deep breath. "My full name is Horatio Alger Huntington-Ackerman. I'm one of the ten richest men in the United States. And until I met you, I was one of the ten unhappiest."

"Horatio Alger Huntington-Ackerman? The chemist and business wizard who invented chemical-free Pensa-Cola, The Thinking Man's Drink? And Damitol, Asylum-Strength Pain Relief Without Side Effects? And Quiche-on-a-Stick? I don't believe you."

"It's true, Mousey. But you have no idea how unhappy all that success and money can make a person if there's no joy in his life, no one to have fun with. I know we can be happy together. I'll do anything in the world for you. Please say you'll marry me."

"No." She was gentle but firm.

"Why not?"

"Because you'd think I was marrying you only for your money and you'd never believe that I really loved you and after a while it would make you sour. I wouldn't marry you unless you were sure I loved you."

"How can I be sure? How can one ever be sure?"

"I could sign something that said I'd never ask for any money from you if we weren't happy together and decided to part."

"Oh, Mousey. *You* are honest and honorable and respectful. All right. Now will you marry me?"

"Yes," Mousey said. Her smile was so dazzling as she looked into Horatio's enraptured face that people dining in the restaurant turned around to see where the light was coming from.

A month later—a month during which Horatio had a two-row theater constructed in his town house—he and Mousey were married in a small ceremony in the garden. The only guests were Bentley and Flossie; Bart and Bernie; and Fleur, Poodles, and Fifi.

Bart and Bernie were furious. Until Horatio married, they were his direct heirs and had always been hopeful that he would work himself into an early grave and spare them the trouble of ever having to earn an honest living. Now that he was married, Mousey and any children they might have would be his heirs. Bart and Bernie wore black to the wedding and glowered and grumbled so much that not even Fleur, Poodles, and Fifi—who knew how to have a good time better than most people—could erase their scowls.

Flossie caught the bouquet and looked at Bentley with misty, sentimental eyes, which made him nervous. With Horatio *and* Mousey to take care of now, he was much too busy to get married, even if the two of them did make marriage seem like a more romantic arrangement than he'd previously believed it to be.

Horatio and Mousey, absorbed totally in each other, noticed nothing except what an excellent day it was to be getting married. The hour before the ceremony, Mousey met with Horatio and his attorneys in the library to sign the papers saying she wanted none of Horatio's money. Instead, Horatio announced to her that because she had proven she loved him by being willing to renounce all his millions, he had decided it was unnecessary for her to sign the papers and everything that was his was now hers, as well.

Mousey wept happy tears before going to change into her wedding dress: white silk trimmed with satin ribbons and rosebuds.

Horatio gave her a fake ermine coat as a wedding present.

CHAPTER

4

For a year Mousey and Horatio lived blissfully in the town house. Their dutiful monthly dinners with Bart and Bernie cast only a fleeting shadow on their happiness. Mousey put on plays, which Horatio and Bentley and Flossie attended. Mousey and Horatio read together in the library. They played long hours of Monopoly, pinochle, hearts, and pool. They found a white kitten in the alley behind the town house and adopted him. They named him Louie and fattened him up on sardines and cream and taught him tricks. He was best at lying down, playing dead, and pretending to be deaf.

One morning Mousey and Horatio sat eating their breakfast at the long polished table in the dining room. They were both sleepy. The burglar alarm had gone off in the town house the night before for the second time in two weeks, scaring them awake. No burglars had been found, but it was disturbing nonetheless.

"Mousey, darling," Horatio said. "I've been thinking. Living in the city isn't nearly what it used to be. It's noisy and dirty and dangerous, and we both prefer to stay home and be with each other instead of going out. My business can be run from anywhere, as long as I have a telephone, a computer, and a fax machine. Why don't we move to the country? We could have a pool and a tennis court and fresh air and sunshine."

Mousey smiled. "I've been thinking that would be a good thing, too," she said in her little voice. "The country is a much nicer place to raise a child."

"But we don't have a child."

"In seven months we will." Mousey smiled her incandescent smile.

Horatio stood up so suddenly his chair fell over backward. Tears of joy filmed his eyes as he gathered Mousey into his arms.

The next morning Horatio and Mousey began their search for the perfect country house.

It turned out to be far harder than they'd thought it would be. The houses that were big enough were ugly. The ones that were pretty enough were too small. And those that were just right weren't for sale.

After weeks of fruitless searching, Horatio said to Mousey, "I've decided that if we're going to get what we want, we'll have to build our own house. So let's look for the perfect *land* instead of the perfect house."

The very next day they found exactly what they

were looking for. At the side of a winding country road, forty miles from the little village of Jupiter, stood a battered old sign that said 33 ACRES FOR SALE. CHEAP. Underneath was a phone number.

Bentley parked the car, and the three of them got out and walked around the property. There were large oak trees spreading their branches over perfect picnic spots. A little brook shimmered between mossy banks, chuckling over the rocks in the streambed. Wildflowers dotted the sunny green acres, and anthems of birdsong filled the air.

Mousey clapped her hands and cried, "It's perfect. I can almost see our house up on that knoll."

"Me, too," Horatio said, and they piled back into the car and drove as fast as they could until they found a phone booth, from which Horatio called the number on the sign. The real estate agent agreed to meet them at the sign in thirty minutes.

"He said it's been for sale a long time," Horatio told Mousey and Bentley as they drove back the way they'd come. "I can't understand why. The price is very reasonable and the place has a perfect building site."

"Maybe because it's so isolated," Mousey suggested. "It *is* forty miles from a grocery store." Because of the life she'd led before she met Horatio, Mousey was much more practical than he.

"Perhaps," Horatio agreed, looking fondly at her and thinking how clever she was.

Before long an old blue car with a dented front fender drove up. A man in a yellow suit and matching shoes got out. He looked first at the Daimler, then at Mousey, and then at Bentley. By the time he focused on Horatio, he was rubbing his hands together.

"My name is Sid Skeet and I'd like to congratulate you folks on your shrewdness. This is the finest parcel of land in three counties. It's buildable, has water, and access by road. The taxes are low, and did you ever breathe such air?"

"How come it's so cheap?" Mousey asked.

Sid Skeet's eyes narrowed. "Shrewder than I thought," he muttered. "This land is owned by Federated Conglomerates. I guess they don't need the money," he said.

"I know all about Federated Conglomerates," Horatio said. "They've never sold anything at a bargain price in their entire corporate history. What's wrong with this land?"

"Well," Skeet said reluctantly, "it's not the land. It's the neighbors. They make some people nervous."

"What neighbors?" Mousey asked.

"Walnut Manor, down the way about a mile," Skeet said. "You can't see it from the road—there are too many trees—but it adjoins this property. Personally, I don't think there's a thing to be concerned about."

"What's Walnut Manor?" Horatio asked.

"Well, it's a looney bin," Sid Skeet said. "But they take only the finest, highest-class wackos. It's too expensive for your lower-class goofballs."

" 'Goofballs'?" Mousey asked with a quaver in her little voice. " 'Wackos'?"

"Tell you what," Sid Skeet said. "If you're really interested in this property, I'll take you over to Walnut Manor and introduce you to Dr. Waldemar. He can show you around, show you what kind of security they have, and all that. It'll set your mind at ease, I can promise you. This is a beautiful piece of land, and I hate to have you nice folks get discouraged about it. Come on, get in your car and follow me. On second thought, why don't I just come along in your car? I've never been in one of these babies."

Before Horatio or Mousey could utter a word of protest, Sid Skeet slid into the backseat, ran his hands over the pecan-burl paneling, the leather seats, the silver bud vases, and twiddled the controls of the sound system. Bentley got stiffly into the driver's seat. Even the back of his neck looked huffy.

Horatio looked at Mousey. They shrugged at each other and joined Sid Skeet in the backseat.

The long curving driveway to Walnut Manor, lined with walnut trees, was impressive. The building itself was equally stately: large, white, pillared, with wings extending out on either side. The driveway continued past the main building to a cluster of smaller white cottages, a large garage, and a stable.

"Behind the building there's a swimming pool and some shuffleboard courts," Skeet said. "The staff lives in those cottages. It's too far to town for them to come and go every day. I promise you, this is where I want to be if I ever go round the bend. But I'd never be able to afford it. Not unless I sell that Fed—" He stopped abruptly. Then, tapping Bentley on the shoulder, he said, "You can park over there." Bentley glided the Daimler into a parking space. "Once you've seen Walnut Acres, maybe I can interest you in the property on the other side of it, too. What do you say?"

"Sorry," Horatio said. "We're only interested in building one house."

Sid Skeet, Mousey, and Horatio entered Walnut Manor. Bentley waited outside.

The first person they encountered in the sumptuous paneled entry hall was a short woman, dressed in a flowered shift pulled down over gray sweatpants. Her outfit was accented by black high-top basketball shoes and a Pensa-Cola baseball cap. She held a bathroom plunger in her hand, and a cigarette dangled from the corner of her mouth.

"Yeah?" she said, looking fiercely at them. Mousey shrank against Horatio and clutched his arm.

Sid Skeet forged ahead. "Where's Dr. Waldemar?" he asked.

The woman turned around, stalked to a heavy paneled door with a brass sign saying OFFICE, opened it, and shouted inside, "Hey, Doc, there're some people out here with Sid Skeet. They look like they can afford the place." She slammed the door, slung the plunger over her shoulder, and headed off down the hall, trailing ashes.

"I thought you said the inmates were high-class here," Mousey squeaked in distress.

"But, darling," Horatio said, "you must admire her taste in baseball hats."

Sid Skeet laughed. "She's no inmate. That's Opal, the custodian. She's got the manners of a train wreck. But Waldemar saves a fortune by having her around. She can do anything: electricity, plumbing, carpentry, furniture moving, tree uprooting, and, in a pinch, she can subdue a violent case."

"I thought there weren't any of those here," Mousey said, looking over her shoulder.

"If there were any," Sid amended, "she could subdue them. But there aren't."

The office door opened, and a short, plump man wearing a gray suit and a distracted air came out. He was mostly bald, with a fringe of white hair circling the back of his head; and he wore round steel-rimmed glasses. "Hello, Sid," he said. "What can I do for you?"

"Hi, Doc. These folks are interested in buying the Federated Conglomerates property adjoining Walnut Manor. They want to check out your security here. Don't want to wake up some morning and find a bunch of nuts in the backyard." Sid Skeet chuckled.

"Oh," Dr. Waldemar said. "Well, let me assure you, there is no possibility of such a thing ever happening. Security here is very, um, secure. Banks could take lessons from us." He gestured to a large panel on the wall full of little TV screens, red lights, and buttons—all with labels under them. They could see themselves on one of the TV screens. "We've never had an escape. Why would anybody want to escape from here, anyway? We like to consider Walnut Manor a sort of private club for our guests. And our guests are from some of the finest families in the country. I'd call them more, um, *distressed* than disturbed. Even if they were to wander off, they would represent absolutely no danger to the public. But why don't I show you around? That should ease your minds. You can wait in the office if you want, Sid. You've seen Walnut Manor plenty of times." As he led Horatio and Mousey down the hall, he said, "We welcome contributions to Walnut Manor from any source, and they are completely tax deductible."

Dr. Waldemar took them first to the dining room. Large windows looked out over the pool and gardens and green lawns, which stopped at the brick wall dividing Walnut Manor from the Federated Conglomerates property. China and silver and crystal were on the tables. As they watched, the kitchen door burst open and Opal shot out carrying a huge plastic bucket of water and ice cubes. She began filling glasses on the tables so quickly she was almost a blur.

They moved on to the library where about twenty people sat playing cards, watching television, reading magazines, and staring at the wall. None of them looked the slightest bit dangerous.

They peered into the neat bedrooms, apparently furnished with some of the patients' own furniture, and into the crafts rooms, before going outdoors to examine the pool, shuffleboard courts, and garden. Everything Horatio and Mousey saw served only to set their minds at ease.

As they walked back to the office, Dr. Waldemar said, "I hope what you've seen would encourage you to send any distressed relative of yours to us should the need ever arise."

They thanked him, but said they doubted such a thing was likely to happen. They collected Sid Skeet from the office and took the Daimler back to Jupiter, where they attended to the paperwork necessary to purchase the land for their new home.

The next few months were busy ones. Horatio and Mousey worked on plans for the house and selected furnishings. Construction began. Mousey often had Bentley drive her out to the site, the Daimler loaded with picnic hampers for the workers. She wanted them cheerful so that they'd work fast, because she intended to bring the baby home from the hospital to the new house.

Horatio was happier than he could remember since he was a child. His businesses ran along without a hitch, and he had lots of time to spend with Mousey, watching her perform her plays, playing games, thinking up names for the baby. When Mousey couldn't find pretty lingerie to accommodate her changing figure, Horatio designed a line of maternity underwear that was frilly and feminine. He called it Mater-Nifties and it was an immediate success. More money rolled in, and Bart and Bernie sat in their dark apartment pounding their idle fists on their fat thighs in frustration. They would have pounded even harder if they had known that all the money from Mater-Nifties rolled right out again to charities benefiting needy children.

One morning Horatio received a phone call from the contractor telling him that his house was finished. That same afternoon he took Mousey to the hospital to have their baby.

For the rest of his life, Horatio remembered that day as the zenith of his personal happiness: The wife he adored presented him with a perfect child; the dream house they had planned together was ready for them to bring their little family to; and he was young, healthy, and wildly happy.

He flew a flag, a big blue one inscribed with IT'S A BOY! from the top of his tallest office building. When he went to see Mousey in the hospital, he was accompanied by a panel truck filled with flowers and candy, not only for Mousey, but for all the other mothers on the maternity floor and all the doctors and nurses.

He found Mousey sitting up in bed looking fresh and radiant and very satisfied with herself.

"Oh, Horatio, isn't he beautiful? He looks just like you."

"Oh, Mousey, my darling!" he exclaimed, kissing her and running off to the nursery. He stood before the glass, tears of wonder and gratitude in his eyes as he gazed at his sleeping son.

Three days later he tenderly gathered Mousey and their still unnamed child into the Daimler, and they drove to their new house in the country.

part two

CHAPTER

5

- - - - - - -

The days and weeks and months flowed easily into one another. Gradually Horatio and Mousey decided there was no reason for them ever to leave their beautiful home. Everything they valued was there.

A high, attractive brick wall surrounded their property. The big iron gate in it stayed locked until visitors had identified themselves through the intercom at the gatepost. Inside the gate were the house, the pool, the tennis court, a stable for the three horses, and a barn for the cow who supplied their milk. There were a few chickens to produce fresh eggs and for Louie—living in a cat's paradise—to chase, and some picturesque ducks who swam in the little brook.

Once in a while, at the beginning, they rode their horses over to the wall that separated them from Walnut Manor and looked over, just to be sure all was in order there. They never saw anything more threatening than a few distracted-looking people, one of whom was sometimes Dr. Waldemar, sitting on the lawn or strolling through the gardens; and eventually they quit thinking about it.

Bentley finally got so lonesome for Flossie that he swallowed his fears and married her, and then wondered why it had taken him so long. She, too, came to live in the country, where she helped with the house and the baby, and tended a vegetable garden outside the kitchen door.

One evening at dinner, Horatio announced that he had decided to name the estate Eclipse.

"Eclipse?" Mousey asked. "Why?"

"Because that's what Bentley does to keep the garden in shape. He clips," Horatio said, laughing.

"But that's such a silly reason," Mousey told him.

"No, that's not why. I'm just teasing you." He took her hand in his. "I'm naming it Eclipse because my new life here with you has so far surpassed my old life in joy and contentment, I can hardly remember it."

"Oh, Horatio," Mousey squeaked. "How beautiful."

Horatio and Mousey quit taking a newspaper because they never found any good news in it. They gave away their television sets because they kept getting bad news on them, too. Horatio called in to his offices once a week, but as long as he left things alone and just allowed the money to make more money, everything went more smoothly than when he was juggling corporations and meeting with his business advisers and tax accountants and worrying about debentures and estoppels and liquidity ratios.

More and more, Horatio and Mousey and Bentley and Flossie spent their time in quiet, peaceful pursuits: reading aloud to one another from the favorite old books; playing games of cards and pool and checkers (Horatio lost his interest in Monopoly); singing to the accompaniment of Mousey's piano and Horatio's guitar; tending to the grounds and the animals; putting on plays; and playing with the baby, whom they had finally named Alexander, because they liked the way his initials spelled AHA, but whom they called Sandy.

The years drifted by in perfect peace and contentment. Sandy learned to swim and ride a horse, to read and play games and make music with his parents. Mousey and Horatio considered sending him to Jupiter to school when he came of school age. But he was such a sweet and generous and likable child that they hated to risk changing that through exposure to other children, and they decided to keep him at home.

The whole family—for Bentley and Flossie were certainly family—participated in Sandy's education, and they all benefited. All of them learned Latin, and one Christmas they translated several Christmas carols into it, not just "Adeste Fidelis," which everybody knows.

To study geography, Horatio ordered an enormous globe, and they all finally found out where Tasmania and Transylvania and Timbuktu and Perth Amboy,

New Jersey, are. Mousey learned long division, which she hadn't understood in fourth grade; and Bentley did chemistry experiments in the butler's pantry, accidently discovering a way to make plastic out of potato peelings. Horatio sold the formula to DuPont for Bentley, which assured Bentley and Flossie's retirement income.

They all learned to diagram sentences and to make pie crust, to spell *cirrostratus nebulosus* (a cloud formation producing a halo phenomenon) and to write haiku, to determine their own blood types and to appreciate Montaigne. Their days were full of sunshine and love and discovery.

The only blot on their otherwise perfect landscape was the third Thursday of every month, when Bart and Bernie came to Eclipse for dinner. All five of them dreaded that day. But they made the best of it and collaborated on an elaborate dinner so there was at least *something* about the evening to enjoy.

These evenings were hard on Bart and Bernie, too. As disagreeable as Horatio's brothers were to start with, the happy atmosphere of Eclipse somehow made them even more odious. They simply could not stand to see people enjoying themselves.

"It's unhealthy for you to bury yourselves out here in the country," they always said. "It's unnatural."

"It's not good for Alexander," they said, "to be deprived of the company of other children. He doesn't act like a regular child."

"Thank goodness," Horatio would reply.

"What do you *do* out here all day long?" they asked. "You're neglecting your businesses."

Horatio and Mousey and Bentley and Flossie and Sandy bit their tongues and gritted their teeth and refrained from arguing with Bart and Bernie. For one thing, they were too polite to argue with their dinner guests, and for another, they didn't want to lower themselves to Bart and Bernie's level.

All of them, except Sandy, of course, knew about smog and traffic jams and computer billing, acid rain and MTV and microwave cooking, the IRS and alarm clocks and soy protein, and they didn't want any more. They were happy in their little utopia, and they didn't care how much that bothered Bart and Bernie.

The years rolled on, each one happier than the one before. Gradually they lost track of time. The batteries in their watches died and weren't replaced. They had no need for calendars. They had no newspaper. They forgot how old they were. What difference did it make?

They never even thought of the future. Each day was perfection enough. Sandy grew taller and more handsome and became a young man, but that was the only chronometer they had. To Horatio, the lines in Mousey's face only made her more dear to him; and she thought the gray in his hair improved his looks.

Bart and Bernie aged, too. The years turned them more churlish than ever because they saw themselves passing into old age without Horatio's fortune to squander. No matter how generous he was with them, they wanted it *all*.

CHAPTER

6

On the third Thursday in September, a crisp fall evening, Bart and Bernie arrived for their monthly dinner with a cake box tied up with string. "We've brought a birthday cake," they announced. "We've noticed that you never celebrate birthdays, and we thought it was time to have a celebration for all of you at once, for all the missed birthday parties."

This was so uncharacteristic of Bart and Bernie that everyone was immediately suspicious. But as the evening wore on and Bart and Bernie remained cheery and pleasant, Horatio and Mousey, too out of practice to remain distrustful, relaxed and smiled with the thought that Bart and Bernie had finally learned to be nice.

Something continued to bother Sandy, though, and he couldn't be at ease. He, who had no experience at all with deceit, deception, and ruthlessness, sensed something odd.

In spite of much urging by Bart and Bernie, he stubbornly refused to have any of the cake. His parents were surprised and disappointed in him for his lack of good manners, but because he had never before behaved strangely without a reason, they trusted his decision.

As usual, they were all relieved when Bart and Bernie, still in high good spirits, left. They sat before the fire with their coffee, once again relishing their solitude and the pleasure of one another's company. Flossie helped Mousey wind some skeins of yarn into balls, and Horatio and Bentley played a game of chess. Sandy sat quietly and stared into the flames, a puzzled look on his face. There was something . . . something. He shook his head and then stared and puzzled some more.

When Sandy awoke the next morning, it was with the sense that something was wrong. He recalled that he had gone to bed with the same feeling. He got up and went to the window, from which every morning he saw Flossie making her inspection tour of the kitchen garden. That morning the garden was empty except for Louie. Old but still remarkably spry, the cat was stalking his favorite chicken—the one they called Attila the Hen—through the scallions.

Odd, thought Sandy. *Maybe Flossie's sleeping late. Or maybe I'm up earlier than usual.* He pulled on his robe and started downstairs.

There was a deeper than usual quality of quiet in the house that morning, a quiet that filled Sandy with foreboding. He paused on the stairs to listen, but there was not a sound. Usually he could hear the clink of

Horatio's coffee cup from the library, where his father liked to start the day by reading something from long ago. Usually he heard the sounds of Bentley and Flossie having breakfast together in the morning room. Usually he heard his mother's bathwater running or her piano or her tinkly laugh.

That morning there was nothing. Sandy ran the rest of the way down the stairs and into the kitchen, which was empty, bright, and clean. Only the remains of the birthday cake, still in its box, disturbed the orderliness. As he stood in the center of the big room, he heard footsteps. Feeling relieved and somewhat foolish, he turned to see Bentley coming through the swinging door to the kitchen. But when he saw the look on Bentley's face, he no longer felt so relieved.

"Something's wrong with Flossie!" Bentley cried. "I can't wake her up. Where's Horatio? Where's Mousey?"

"They're not up yet," Sandy said. "But I think we should wake them." He grabbed Bentley by the arm and they ran up the stairs to Horatio and Mousey's room. They knocked on the door, got no response, knocked harder, then shouted. But still there was no reply.

Sandy opened the door, and he and Bentley rushed across the pale green carpet of the big, airy room, fragrant with the great bouquets of flowers Mousey loved, to the bedside. Horatio and Mousey lay side by side, breathing quietly, pink cheeked and bemused looking, despite their closed eyes.

They would not wake up. Bentley and Sandy shook them and yelled into their ears. Bentley even slapped

Horatio's face, the way he had seen it done in old movies, but nothing worked.

"This is exactly how Flossie is," Bentley said, defeated. "She looks just like she's sleeping. She doesn't seem to be in pain and she doesn't look sick. She just won't wake up."

"Let me see her," Sandy said.

They made their way to the other wing of the house, where Flossie and Bentley had their quarters.

Flossie was exactly as Bentley had described her, exactly as Horatio and Mousey were.

"Do you think it's all right to move her?" Sandy asked Bentley. "Because I think we should put them all together. It'll be easier to watch over them. And we've got to call Dr. Malcolm."

"Good idea," Bentley said. Gingerly he tried to lift Flossie, but she had become so plump from her own good cooking, he needed Sandy's help to carry her to Mousey and Horatio's room.

They arranged Flossie on the chaise longue and covered her with a quilt. Then they tried again to waken the three sleepers but were again unsuccessful.

Together they went to the kitchen, where Bentley started a pot of coffee while Sandy called the doctor. As they sat at the kitchen table drinking coffee and waiting for the doctor, they watched Attila strutting around the kitchen, pecking hopefully at the pattern on the linoleum, and clucking flirtatiously at Louie, whom she had followed in through the cat door.

"Do you want any breakfast?" Bentley asked Sandy.

"I couldn't eat a thing. Looks like Attila's the only one with an appetite." He took a saucer from the cupboard and crumbled some of the leftover birthday cake into it. He set it on the floor, where Louie sniffed it disdainfully and flopped down under the table. Attila happily ate it all, while Sandy put the rest of the cake down the disposal.

"No need to save this," he said to Bentley. "Nothing to celebrate now."

When Dr. Malcolm arrived, Bentley and Sandy took him upstairs to see the patients. After giving them a thorough examination and asking Bentley and Sandy a lot of questions, he scratched his head.

"I'm mystified," he admitted. "I've been coming out here once a year for I-don't-know-how-many-years, giving you all your shots and your physicals, and I've never seen such a healthy bunch. I decided this unorthodox lifestyle must agree with you. A dose of it'd probably do me some good, too. Might help this little touch of neuralgia I have—"

Bentley cleared his throat pointedly.

"Oh, yes. Well, I can't find anything obviously wrong with them. They seem to be in light comas, but I can't figure out why. Might be some kind of virus you two are immune to. I'll have to put them in the hospital to do some tests."

"Do they have to go to the hospital?" Sandy asked. "They haven't left here in years. They love it here. If they're going to get better, they'll do it here and not in the hospital. And if they aren't going to get better . . ." He swallowed hard. "Well, I know they'd rather be here in that case, too. We can get hospital beds and hire nurses or whatever it takes. Please."

"Well, I suppose that's possible. It'll take a lot of arranging, though," Dr. Malcolm said reluctantly. "And I'll have to be running out here all the time."

"We'll pay you double," Sandy said. "And Bentley and I will help. Please."

Using the phone in Mousey's little office next to the bedroom, Dr. Malcolm made the arrangements for turning the spacious master bedroom into a sickroom.

"The nurse should be here in a couple of hours," Dr. Malcolm said, walking down the front staircase. "And I'll be back later in the afternoon to start the tests. Just keep an eye on them." He went out to his car.

"I think we should take some sandwiches and coffee upstairs. We can watch over them until the nurse comes," Bentley said. "I'm finally hungry."

They went to the kitchen, where Bentley picked up Attila's empty saucer and put it in the dishwasher before he started to make chicken sandwiches (not from any-one Attila knew). Sandy packed the picnic basket with a thermos of coffee and some fruit.

Louie came out from under the kitchen table where he and Attila had been snoozing together. He stretched thoroughly and went to sit patiently on Bentley's right foot until he was given a piece of chicken. Then he sauntered through the cat door to lie outside in the sun on the patio.

"Hey!" Sandy called after him. "You forgot your girlfriend." He bent down to where Attila slept. "Come on, sleeping beauty," he said. "You can't stay in here without Louie." He shook her but nothing happened.

"What is it?" Bentley asked, turning from his sandwiches.

"It's Attila. Now I can't wake *her* up."

Bentley dropped the bread knife and crouched under the kitchen table with Sandy. They shook her, but Attila, like Mousey, Horatio, and Flossie, would not wake.

Sandy sat back on his heels. "What in the world is going on here?" He looked desperately around the kitchen, as if there was something dangerous in the very air of the house. Then he looked hard at the dishwasher and stood up. "Bentley, did you have any of that birthday cake last night?"

"Of course not. I rarely eat sweets; you know that. And I certainly wouldn't eat anything *those* characters brought."

Sandy smacked his forehead with the palm of his hand. "That's it! The birthday cake. All four of them ate the cake. We didn't."

Bentley stood up. "You mean you think Bart and Bernie tried to . . . poison us all?"

"Yes, I do. That's the only way this makes sense. They've been after Horatio's fortune for years, the lazy good-for-nothings. Remember how hard they tried to convince you and me to have a piece of cake last night? How they kept insisting it was the best cake ever made and it was a party and we were being spoilsports by not having any? If their plan had worked, it would have looked like an epidemic of food poisoning. Lord knows how long it would have been before anybody found us. And I just destroyed the evidence. How could I have been so stupid?"

"You're not stupid," Bentley said, alarmed. "You figured out what Bart and Bernie are up to. They would have been Horatio's only heirs. And now, you're still in the way of what they want."

"You're right," Sandy said, getting to his feet. "I've got to be very careful now. I wonder how long they'll be able to resist trying to find out how we all are."

The phone rang. Bentley picked up the kitchen extension and said, "Eclipse. Bentley here."

There was a long silence on the other end. Then a click and the hum of the dial tone.

"Guess who," Sandy said.

"What do we do now?" Bentley asked.

"We're going to pretend everything's fine until we know how Flossie and Horatio and Mousey are. Come on. Let's get upstairs. We've got to take even better care of them now that we know what's going on."

They made a nest of dish towels in a plastic dishpan, put Attila gently into it, and carried her upstairs to the sickroom. There they sat, eating sandwiches and watching their patients breathing serenely in and out.

7

They jumped when the doorbell rang, announcing the simultaneous arrival of the nurse and the van carrying the hospital equipment.

"Hi. I'm Sunnie Stone. I'm supposed to be the nurse," said the glorious creature standing on the doorstep. The sun made a nimbus of her silvery blond hair. "I mean, I *am* the nurse. I just finished my training last week and I can't get used to actually being one yet. I hope you don't mind. I haven't had a lot of experience, but Dr. Malcolm said there wasn't much to do for the patients, since they're just lying in bed like turnips . . . I mean, oh dear, I'm not doing very well, am I?"

"What?" Sandy asked, dazzled by her radiance.

She peered at him. "I'm the nurse," she said slowly. "I've come to help with the patients."

"Oh, yes, of course," Sandy said, realizing that he had missed out on something important through the years he had lived at Eclipse. "Please come in. Let me take your luggage." He grabbed the handle of the large brown suitcase but could barely lift it. He set it down again for a better grip. "What have you got in here?"

"Books," she said. "I've worked all my life, from the time I was a little girl, and I never had time to read any books except in school. Now that I'm finally educated, I want to improve my mind. I know that sounds funny, but maybe you know what I mean. Dr. Malcolm said I'd probably have a lot of time on my hands here because the patients don't require too much in the way of actual nursing care, so I thought I could probably get some reading done." While she talked, Sandy dragged the suitcase into the hall to make room for Bentley to supervise the moving in of the hospital equipment. "It was a real challenge trying to decide what to read," Sunnie went on. "I got a list of the Harvard Classics from my librarian and I thought I would just start at the top and read all the way through them. But do you know what the first three books on the list are? *The Autobiography of Benjamin Franklin*, *The Journal of John Woolman*, and *Fruits of Solitude*. I didn't feel like reading any of those, so I asked the librarian for a suggestion and she told me *War and Peace*. I started it, and in the first chapter there were twenty-two characters' names! I was too confused to keep reading, so I decided to read by subject matter and learn all about one thing at a time. I started with whales. Don't ask me why. First, I read an article in the encyclopedia. It was pretty interesting, too. Did you know whales are cetaceans and they travel in pods? But when I came to the . . ."—she blushed prettily—"the sperm whales, I had to stop. Did you know there's a whale novel? It's called *Moby Dick*. I liked it but I sure know more about whaling than I hope I'll ever need to know. The encyclopedia made whales seem much nicer than Herman Melville does." She sighed. "Anyway, my suitcase is full of whale books, but I don't know . . . Maybe I should have started with something a little more . . . familiar. You know what I mean?"

Sandy's eyes had taken on a glazed look as he listened to Sunnie. There was a silence before he said, "Oh, uh, yes. Yes, I know what you mean. I've read *Moby Dick*." He looked around and found the men from the hospital supply were just leaving. He realized guiltily that, for a few moments, he'd forgotten all about Horatio and Mousey and Flossie and Attila. "Let me show you the patients," he said, lugging the suitcase up the stairs. "We'll fix a bedroom for you in the office next to the sickroom."

When Sandy dragged Sunnie's suitcase into Mousey's office, he found that Bentley had already moved a bed into it. The hospital-supply men had taken the regular bedroom furniture into another wing, and three hospital beds lined one wall. Attila's dishpan rested on an enamel table next to Mousey's bed, and cartons of medical supplies were piled in corners.

Sunnie went to each patient's bedside and took temperatures, pulses, and blood pressures. "Everything looks normal," she said. "Except for the comas, of course. This is the first time I ever took a chicken's pulse, and I certainly don't know what's a normal pulse for a chicken. But she's still breathing, and that's what counts in the long run. In the short run, too, if you really think about it." She turned her round blue eyes on Sandy. "Since everything seems under control here for the moment, I think I'll unpack. I didn't know how long I'd be here, so I brought a lot."

"I noticed," Sandy said.

Late in the afternoon Dr. Malcolm arrived and, with Sunnie's help, conducted every test he could think of on the patients. Each test eventually came back normal. And still, mysteriously, the sleepers slept.

Sandy could be thankful only that Bart and Bernie had miscalculated the amount of whatever they'd put into the cake so that it hadn't been lethal. And he knew he'd never forgive himself for putting the rest of the cake down the disposal. Without it as evidence, no one would believe what he knew to be true.

The days unfolded into a new routine of meals, patient care, and walks—for exercise and tension relief, rather than for pleasure—through the grounds of Eclipse. Sunnie was a perfect nurse, caring and tender, and she lived up to her name in disposition. The odd little household accommodated the altered style of their lives, but Sandy, and Bentley, too, missed more than they could say the old life of shared work and play and enlightenment.

Knowing Sunnie was an unexpected adventure for Sandy. She represented the outside world for him, a world which, though he knew it existed, had seemed so distant and imaginary as to be irrelevant. Suddenly it was here, in his own home.

"You know, Sandy," Sunnie said one day as they walked through the gardens scattering crumbs for the chickens, "I can see why you never wanted to leave here."

"I never thought about it," he said honestly. "Leaving here simply never occurred to me."

"Well, if it ever does, I'd suggest ignoring it. You have no idea how restorative it is for me to be here. The bustle of the city, the hassles of living there . . . why, it's a jungle. I've worked hard from the time I was a little girl, and this is the first vacation I've ever had. Oh, I realize it's not a *real* vacation. I mean, I know I'm working, but it's so nice and easy here. My mother wasn't very well and I never knew my father, so I had to take care of a lot of things. My mother was an actress, but she had to leave the only good role she ever got when she found I was on the way. My father was a street juggler who went to Florida in the winters. Because of the weather, you know. He left just before I was born, and he didn't come back when he'd said he would. In fact, he never came back. For years my mother spent her days walking around the streets looking for him, hoping he'd returned without telling her, the way a charming but irresponsible rogue, which he was, would do. That's probably what broke down her health, so much walking around in all kinds of weather. Then when her health got too poor for her to walk, she sat at home looking out the window of our apartment, still watching for him." Sunnie lowered her voice. "She used to drink a little more than was really good for her.

"Even when I was small I earned a little money running errands for some of the other people in the apartment house. I'd go to the market for them or walk their dogs or buy a newspaper for them. We were always short of money. Then when I was old enough, I got real jobs after school, waitressing and working in the dime store and things like that. But my mother was getting sicker and sicker, and I spent a lot of time taking care of her. That's when I decided to be a nurse. I really liked taking care of her. But she died anyway. I mean, I don't think the way I took care of her had anything to do with it," she said hastily. "I think she would have died no matter who was taking care of her. But the oddest thing was, right after she died, I got a telegram from a lawyer in Florida telling me my father had just died and left me and my mother some money. He'd stayed in Florida all that time, and had a little nightclub. I was really mad at him. But then I found out from the lawyer how my father had always felt guilty about leaving me and my mother but he just wasn't cut out to be a family man. Then I wasn't quite so mad. I mean, it was an awful thing to do to us, but it bothered him for the rest of his life, so he wasn't as hard-hearted as I thought. Nobody's simple, I guess. So anyway, I took the money he left me. It was just enough to support me so I didn't have to work at anything except school, and the day the money ran out was the day Dr. Malcolm called and asked me to come here. So things work out.

They really do. Now I can support myself doing something I love to do, and my very first assignment is in this lovely place taking care of your sweet family. Oh, I know they're sweet. I can tell from the way they smile in their sleep. I've even become fond of Attila. Look how poor Louie misses her. Every morning after breakfast he comes upstairs and gets in the dishpan with her for a while. I'll bet she knows it, too, even in her sleep. That's why I talk to your parents and Flossie all the time I'm taking care of them. In nursing school we learned that the last sense to go is hearing and that it's important to talk to our patients all the time, even if we don't think they can hear us. I always try to be encouraging when I talk to them. I tell your mother and father and Flossie that someday they're going to wake up, and the first thing they'll want is a hug and the next thing they'll want is a steak. You have to feed both hungers, you know. I'm not sure exactly what to tell Attila. I mean, I don't know if chickens need much hugging, and I feel funny telling her I'll have a big fat bug ready for her when she wakes up. But that's what I tell her, just in case she can understand me."

They had walked for several miles around Eclipse while Sunnie talked, but Sandy hardly noticed. He never tired of listening to her talk, and she had so much to say. She made him think about things he had never considered before, such as the hunger for hugs as well as for steaks. And how a runaway husband and father could suffer from what he had done, too. And lots of other things as well.

As entranced as he was by Sunnie, Sandy's days were still shadowed by the continued absence of those in the sickroom. Every morning he woke with the hope that this day might be the one when life returned to normal. But it never was.

CHAPTER

8

- - - - - - -

One evening as Bentley and Sandy sat in the kitchen trying to decide whether they should make pea soup or toasted cheese sandwiches for supper, and Sunnie sat upstairs watching over the patients, the intercom buzzer sounded. Bentley and Sandy looked questioningly at each other, and then Bentley went to answer it. Sandy trailed along behind him.

"Yes?" Bentley said into the intercom.

"It's Bart and Bernie," said a loud voice. "Tonight's the third Thursday of October. It's time for our monthly dinner. Open the gate."

Sandy and Bentley looked at each other, aghast. They'd forgotten all about the monthly dinner.

"What shall I say?" Bentley whispered frantically.

Sandy stepped up to the intercom, trying to control his rage. "We forgot this was the night," he said. "You know, without calendars, it's hard to keep track. Let's skip this month. I promise we won't forget next time."

"No problem," Bart yelled into the microphone. "We'll take potluck. Open the gate."

"Well, to tell the truth, we've all had a touch of the flu. We're probably still contagious. I certainly wouldn't want you to catch it."

"We're disgustingly healthy," Bart bellowed. "Don't worry. Open the gate."

"Disgusting, anyway," Sandy muttered.

"What?" Bart yelled.

"Nothing. So we'll see you next month, OK?" Sandy said, hoping they'd get the idea.

"If you don't open this gate," Bart hollered, "we'll have to assume something worse than the flu is wrong and we'll have to let the board of directors of HAHA, Inc. know. And they'll be out here before you know what happened, with court orders and habeas corpuses and stuff like that, just to be sure Horatio's of sound mind, et cetera. So open the gate."

"We're going to have to let them in," Sandy said. "Act as if everything's fine. We may even have to feed them. Just don't eat *anything* they've touched." He pressed the intercom button and said, "OK, I'll open the gate. But Mousey and Flossie and Horatio have already gone to bed, so you'll have to be content to eat with just me and Bentley."

"Perfect," Bart said, and laughed evilly.

When the doorbell rang, Bentley cautiously opened the door.

"Evening, Bentley old boy," Bart said, stepping over

the threshold and thumping Bentley's shoulder so hard he nearly knocked him over. "Come on, Bernie. Don't just stand out there freezing." Bernie came in and closed the door behind him.

Sandy restrained his impulse to leap at them both and . . . and . . . well, he didn't know exactly what, but it would be bad. Then his better judgment reasserted itself, and he knew that if he was ever to prove their responsibility for what had happened to his parents and Flossie, he had to keep his wits about him.

Bernie thrust a bottle of wine into Bentley's hands. "We brought this to have with dinner. The least we could do."

Bentley held the bottle at arm's length, only his thumb and forefinger touching it around the neck. It was port, which he despised, and not a very good year, at that.

"While you whip us up some dinner," Bart said, throwing his overcoat, and then Bernie's, over Bentley's outstretched arm, "I'll run up and have a look at my dear brother." He crossed to the staircase.

Sandy grabbed his flabby arm. "I told you he's gone to sleep. You can't wake him up."

For a moment they stood looking each other directly in the eyes, and Sandy knew they each could read the other's thoughts. Bart knew something was wrong with Horatio. And Bart knew Sandy understood his and Bernie's parts in what was wrong. War was silently declared.

"I'll see him next time, then. Won't I?" he asked Sandy challengingly as he turned from the stairs.

"Absolutely," Sandy said grimly.

Bentley said, "We were just going to open a can of soup for supper."

"A can of soup is dandy with us," Bart said. "Right, Bernie? And this bottle of wine will make it a real party." He strode off to the kitchen.

Sandy grabbed Bentley's arm and whispered, "Let's just feed them and get them out of here."

Bentley put together a plate of toasted cheese sandwiches and started the soup heating on the stove.

Bart said, "I'll go wash my hands and then I'll open the wine." He left the kitchen and a minute later they heard a scream from upstairs.

Bentley, Sandy, and Bernie ran up the stairs and found Sunnie at the door of the sickroom, her arms stretched across the entrance, screaming her head off as Bart tried to get past her.

"What are you doing up here?" Sandy yelled, grabbing Bart by the collar and pulling him away from where he hovered threateningly over Sunnie.

"I just wanted to tiptoe up and see my own brother," Bart said, shrugging Sandy off, pushing Sunnie aside, and marching possessively into the sickroom. "How come you need a nurse and hospital beds and all this other junk if they've only got the flu? What's this chicken doing in here? I want my own doctor to examine them, and I'm going to inform my lawyer about this, too." Bart cast triumphant glances at Sandy as he spoke. "Your father has a fortune to manage, and if he's incompetent to do it, as it certainly looks like he is, I want something done about it, and done in a hurry. I always knew this was an unhealthy setup, the way you live out here like hermits, getting more and more re- moved from reality. Wouldn't surprise me if you were all crazy as bedbugs. And I doubt I'd have any trouble convincing a court of that."

He and Bernie bustled down the stairs and out into the night, slamming the heavy front door behind them.

Then Bentley and Sandy had to explain to Sunnie who Bart and Bernie were, and why they were so dan- gerous.

At nine the next morning, Bart and Bernie were back at the front gate, this time with a doctor and a lawyer and a court order. There was nothing Sandy or Bentley could do to prevent them from coming in.

The doctor examined the patients, read Sunnie's me- ticulous records, and determined that the patients were in comas, had been that way for a month, and that nobody knew why. Bart insisted the circumstances were questionable, to say the least, and he cast elaborately accusing looks at Bentley, Sandy, and Sunnie.

As he left, the lawyer said to Sandy, "You'll be hear- ing from me. Your uncles are going to bring some kind of charges. They say you're the only one who stands to gain by your parents' death or incapacitation."

Sandy turned to Bentley after the door had closed

and said, "He thinks I had something to do with the comas."

"Don't you think that would be the first thing Bart would suggest? And Bernie will agree with anything Bart says."

"But why would I? I've got everything I want right here. Nobody would believe I tried to kill them."

"What if Bart said you hated living out here, so isolated? That you wanted to go back into the world and live a different life and your parents wouldn't let you go? Then somebody might believe it."

Sandy pounded his fist on the newel post. "I'd never think of such a thing," he said, rubbing his bruised fist. "But, of course, Bart and Bernie would. What can we do?"

Bentley had been away from the world too long to remember much about wheeling and dealing. "We'll have to think," he said helplessly.

They went upstairs to sit in the sickroom with Sunnie. There was comfort in her presence, and they felt a need, as well, to be near those they loved most in the world—the ones whose suffering they shared and whose plight broke their hearts.

The next day Sandy received, by special messenger, a summons demanding his presence at a hearing having to do with his father's condition. He knew he had to go: He needed to clear his name. But he also knew he couldn't reveal the dastardliness of Bart and Bernie and accuse them of attempted murder unless he had some proof of what they had done. It was going to be intolerable to face them in the courtroom knowing what they had done and knowing that they knew he knew and not being able to say anything about them.

While Bentley sat with the sleepers, Sandy walked in the gardens with Sunnie. The pale, watery sunlight offered no warmth and the trees were bare.

Sunnie patted Sandy's arm. "Try not to worry. Things almost always work out, and they will this time, too. You'll see. Who could believe you'd try to do anything to your darling parents? Anyway, if you wanted them out of the way, why would you go to all the trouble of taking such good care of them now? Why wouldn't you just let them . . . go?"

"You're right! If I'd poisoned them, I wouldn't be trying to save them now. Oh, Sunnie, you've probably saved my life. How can I thank you?"

"You don't have to thank me. Saving lives is a nurse's job. Anyway, just getting to know you and Bentley and your sweet family is the best thing that's ever happened to me, and I want your family to wake up as much as you do. You know, I was wondering if some vitamins might help them. Of course, the liquid nutrition they're getting is full of vitamins, but everybody's vitamin requirements are different, and when you're sick you have different requirements than usual. I think a lot of illnesses, even mental ones, might be connected with lack of vitamins. And our food these days, well, my goodness, it's been so processed and fiddled with, it's a wonder there are any vitamins left in it at all. If there were any to start with, after it's been grown in the strange soil we have now, what with chemical wastes and all. I remember reading a study in nursing school about rats that were fed cereal—just everyday breakfast cereal—and other rats that were fed the cereal *box* all ground up. Believe it or not, the ones that ate the box did better than the ones that ate the cereal. I quit eating cereal after that. But it certainly makes breakfast difficult. Bacon and eggs have so much cholesterol, and cereal, well, I just told you about that. And there's something so lonesome about a plain piece of toast. Breakfast has been a real problem for me since I learned so much. You know, whales have the right idea. They just swim along with their mouths open and whatever floats in is what they eat. Sperm whales—there, you see, I got used to calling them that—eat mostly squid. Can you imagine being so picky? But squid beaks may be what cause the production of ambergris in the whale's intestines, and that's what they make perfume from. So it all works out, just like I told you. I think I know enough about whales, but I can't decide what my next subject should be. What would you like to know if you were me?"

Sandy laughed. Lately, only Sunnie could make him do that. "I can't pretend to imagine how your mind works, Sunnie. I don't think there's another one like it in the whole world. *I* want to know what to say at that hearing."

"You'll know because it'll come straight from your heart, and that's where anything that means anything at all always comes from. You love your parents and Flossie, and even Attila, and it shows, so don't worry about that. Save your worrying for Bart and Bernie. They must want that money in the worst way."

"I hope their ways don't get any worse than they already are," Sandy said.

The day before the hearing, Bentley took the ancient Daimler out of the garage and washed it. He rarely drove it anymore because everything they needed was delivered.

He brushed his chauffeur's uniform, which had hung unused in his closet for years, and polished the bill of the cap. He would be driving Sandy into the city, a place he could hardly remember.

The next morning Sandy, dressed in his best and looking very handsome, got into the front seat of the Daimler beside Bentley. They pulled solemnly out of the driveway as Sunnie stood on the broad front steps and waved good-bye until she could no longer see them.

It was a long and nerve-racking day for Sunnie. She spent her time moving from one bedside to another, holding hands with her patients, and talking to them. Louie, as if aware of her agitation, spent the whole day in the sickroom, too, migrating from bed to bed for a succession of naps.

"I know no hospital would permit a cat to sleep with the patients," Sunnie told him, "but if I had my own hospital, I'd allow it. There's a lot of things I'd do if I had my own hospital. I'd paint the walls bright colors, for one thing. I don't know why beige is so popular. If I were sick, I'd want to be cheered up, not bored silly. And I'd keep the rooms warm. I don't know why hospital rooms are always so cold. Those little cotton blankets they give you are never enough to keep you really warm and cozy. And I wouldn't hire anybody who didn't have a positive reverence for life and for people's feelings. When people are sick, they're *sick,* and they're entitled to be grouchy or whiny. They shouldn't have to try to be nice if they're in pain, and they shouldn't have to wait for half an hour for a bedpan or to have their beds straightened up. Honestly, you wouldn't believe some of the things I saw during my training. It made me wonder why some of those people were in nursing school at all."

Louie yawned and settled himself next to Flossie's feet.

Daylight was fading into early winter darkness when Sunnie and Louie finally heard the Daimler crunching over the gravel in the circular driveway. Sunnie stood in the hall at the top of the stairs where she could look into the sickroom and also down into the entry hall. As soon as she heard the door open, she called down, "What happened? What happened?"

Sandy looked up at her and, though she couldn't see his face in the shadows of the hall, the slump of his shoulders told her that he didn't have good news.

"What *is* it?" Sunnie asked, when Sandy got to the top of the stairs.

"I'm incompetent."

"What?"

"Not only did the judge declare Horatio incompetent to manage his affairs—*I* could have told him that—but he declared me incompetent, too. There were two whole tables full of Horatio's lawyers in the courtroom, including the distinguished Senior Partner, but none of them could change the fact that I don't know one thing about managing our financial affairs."

Sunnie grabbed his cold hands. "Does this mean Bart and Bernie get the money?"

"No. Not yet. Horatio and Mousey are alive, and so am I, so it's still ours. But I don't get control of it."

"Well, who does?"

"Can we sit down?" Sandy asked. "This has been a long and horrible day, and I'm exhausted."

"Of course." She kept hold of one of his hands as they walked into the sickroom. "Where's Bentley?"

"Putting the car away. He said he'd bring dinner up. We stopped at a deli on the way home and got some food. Have you ever been to a deli?"

"Sure. Lots of times. Oh, Sandy, I keep forgetting you don't know anything about real life."

"That's why I'm incompetent. That deli was the only good thing that happened all day. The smells! The people! Salamis hanging from the ceiling and a crock full of wonderful pickles and a loaf of bread in the shape of an alligator. There was an old lady wearing a T-shirt that said NUKE THE WHALES—oh, I'm sorry, I forgot about your whales—but I never saw anything like it. There was a man who looked just like the picture of Jesus in the Bible. He was sitting on the sidewalk outside the deli. I wanted to go talk to him, but Bentley wouldn't let me. What if he really *was* Jesus?"

"I'm pretty sure he wasn't," Sunnie said, settling Sandy into an armchair.

"The whole ride through the city was something. The noise, and all the cars and people and buildings. How does everybody know what to do and where to go? It looked so confusing and scary. And exciting, all at the same time. But I didn't see any jungle, like you said was there. I was lucky, I guess."

Bentley came into the sickroom straining under the weight of a loaded tray. Louie hopped out of Attila's dishpan, where he had been napping, and twined himself around Bentley's ankles. Sandy picked him up and struggled to hold him until Bentley put the tray down. Then he opened a can of sardines that occupied Louie while Bentley unwrapped huge, oily, pungent packages of sandwiches.

When they were finally all settled with their food, Sunnie asked, "Now will somebody please tell me what happened?"

Sandy looked at Bentley. "You tell her."

Bentley said, "The court appointed some of Horatio's lawyers as conservators of the estate. The situation will be reviewed annually, or any time something changes. Like if Horatio wakes up. Or Sandy learns to manage things. But at least Bart and Bernie won't get their hands on the money. Oh, I wish you could have seen their faces. They were so mad. They thought they were going to make it look like Sandy had tried to do his parents in, just the way we thought they would. But we were ready for them, thanks to you, Sunnie. You'd have to be an idiot not to see that Sandy is trying to save his parents, not get rid of them."

Sunnie licked olive oil off her fingers. "Well, that's not so bad, Sandy."

"Tell her the rest," Sandy said.

"What rest?" she asked.

"The rest is, the court decided we can't keep Horatio, Mousey, and Flossie here. The judge said that for their own safety, they should be in a place where there's a doctor available. Nothing we could say would change the judge's mind. We have a week to move them." He looked glumly into his bottle of celery tonic. "Flossie and I have spent every night since we were married under the same roof. I can't imagine what I'll do without her."

"Where are you going to move them?" Sunnie asked.

"I don't know. We have to start looking for a place. Do you know of a good place, Sunnie? One close to Eclipse, so we can see them every day?"

"They gave us a book in nursing school that lists facilities like that. Let me get it." She went into Mousey's little office and came back with a thick blue book. She flipped the pages until she came to their county, and then began running her finger down the columns. "Nope, too far . . . too far . . . too crummy, I know that place . . . too far . . . hey! What's the name of the road Eclipse is on?"

"Old Country Road," Sandy said. "Why?"

"Well, there's a convalescent home located on Old Country Road. There're an M.D. and an R.N. in residence. It's not too big—in fact it's real small. Let me see . . . it's got a swimming pool—not that our patients care—but it sounds nice, and it's . . . Wow, it's expensive, but what do we care? Three hot meals, recreational activities, separate wing for isolation patients. Sounds terrific."

"What's the name of this place?" Sandy asked.

"Walnut Manor."

"Walnut Manor?" Bentley asked. "That's right next door. I thought it was a funny farm, not a convalescent hospital."

"It says here that they take 'the patient needing only minimal medical care. Our primary concern is the temporarily distressed patient.' What does that mean, I wonder? Plenty of times I've been temporarily distressed."

"Who cares what it means?" Bentley said. "It's perfect. Our sleepers certainly need only minimal care, and they'd be right next door. We could spend almost as much time with them as we do now."

"Don't you think we should visit, just to make sure it's as good as it sounds?" Sandy asked.

"I've been there," Bentley said. "A long time ago, just before Horatio bought this land. We wanted to be sure the patients weren't dangerous, living right next door to us. They certainly haven't been. In all the years we've lived here, we've only had one incident with a patient from there. This was when Sandy was still a toddler. I was out exercising the horses, before we got rid of them and got bicycles instead, and I was riding over by the wall. There was a kite stuck in the big walnut tree on our side of the wall, and the string went down on the other side. I heard this awful crying, so I rode right up to the wall and looked over. A man was sitting on the ground holding the kite string and bawling his head off. 'My kite, my kite,' he was crying in this little baby voice. 'I want my kite back.' And then suddenly he'd stop crying and say in a very grown-up voice, 'It's only a kite. We can get another one. Don't cry.' And then he'd start crying all over again. He looked up and saw me watching him, and he popped his thumb in his mouth. When I offered to help him get his kite back, he pulled out his thumb and said in his grown-up voice, 'Oh, could you? He'd appreciate it so much.' Then he stuck his thumb back in his mouth. I got the kite down and handed it over the wall, and he said, 'Thank you ever so much. How very kind of you. Say thank you, Boom-Boom.' Then he put his thumb back in and this sound sort of like 'thank you' came out around the thumb, and he took his kite and walked off."

"Sounds harmless enough," Sunnie said, "but I think we should go over there tomorrow. If it looks as good as it sounds, it should be perfect." Then she looked doleful. "I'll sure miss my patients. And this beautiful house. I was so lucky to have this for my first nursing assignment. I'll never forget any of you."

As Sandy helped Bentley carry the supper things downstairs he said, "Maybe . . . maybe we could still keep a private duty nurse once we move Horatio and Mousey and Flossie and Attila. I mean, four more patients, that's a lot . . . And Sunnie's such a wonderful nurse. And so interesting to talk to. Even Louie loves her."

Bentley looked at Sandy and remembered his own youth, when he was first courting Flossie. Living at Eclipse for so many years hadn't given him amnesia. He recalled what infatuation felt like, and he recognized it on Sandy's face.

CHAPTER

9

In the morning, they drew straws to see who got to go to Walnut Manor and who stayed home with the patients. Sandy and Sunnie drew the long straws, so Bentley got a chemistry textbook and a thermos of coffee and settled himself in the overstuffed chair in the sickroom. Sunnie changed out of her uniform while Sandy waited in the front hall.

"Hurry, Sunnie!" he called up the stairs.

"I'm coming, I'm coming," she said, taking one last look at her patients. She scratched Louie behind the ears, waved to Bentley, and finished fastening the belt on her gray wool dress as she ran down the stairs.

"Oh," he said. "You look so different in clothes." He blushed. "I mean, out of your uniform. No, not like that. I mean, that's a pretty dress."

Sunnie laughed. "I know what you mean. Thank you. Shall we go?"

They put on their coats and gloves and went down the wide front steps to the driveway, where two bicycles waited. They rode through the gates of Eclipse, and Sunnie waited while Sandy locked them again. October chill pinked their cheeks as they pedaled the mile up Old Country Road to Walnut Manor.

Stately, leafless trees lined the curving drive to Walnut Manor. They parked their bicycles at the foot of the steps leading to the broad porch of the main building. Sunnie said, "You'd better let me do the talking. I know more about this than you do."

"Okay," Sandy said, gawking at the big building. It was handsome in an unkempt way, without the grace and tidiness of Eclipse. "It needs painting."

"Winter's the wrong time to paint," Sunnie said. "You do that in the spring or the summer, when the weather's better."

"We paint at Eclipse when things need painting," Sandy told her. He pointed up to the third floor. "There's a broken window up there."

"I'm sure they'll get around to fixing it," Sunnie said. "You mustn't let your reluctance to move our sleepers prejudice you against a good place. Give it a chance, Sandy."

"You're right," he said contritely. "I'll try."

"That's the right attitude," she said, and patted his arm. She started up the steps, while he stood transfixed by the way his arm tingled where she had touched him.

"Come *on,*" Sunnie said over her shoulder.

Sandy hurried up the steps and through the heavy door into the main hall.

Inside it was absolutely silent. The hardwood floors

gleamed softly, and the aroma of lemon oil and coffee and cigarette smoke floated in the air. There were two closed doors on either side of the hall, and beyond them the hall opened into a big square area with a staircase rising from it on the left. Straight across the square area a set of double doors opened into a dining room with windows all across the back looking out to the pool. Opposite the staircase was another set of double doors, which were closed.

Sandy looked at Sunnie. "Nice and quiet," he whispered encouragingly.

Sunnie nodded and went to the door labeled OFFICE. She opened it, peered in, and motioned for Sandy to follow. Behind a counter was a typewriter on a desk and another closed door. From behind the door came the muffled sounds of people talking. Only an occasional word was intelligible. They heard "bacon" and "laundry" and something that sounded like "cat molester."

Sunnie rang the bell on the counter. At its sound, the voices behind the door ceased. There was a long pause, and then the door flew open as if it had been kicked. A figure in a flowered shift over gray sweatpants burst out. She wore high-top basketball shoes and a white nurse's cap, and a cigarette with a long ash hung from the corner of her mouth. She carried a screwdriver.

"Yeah?" she said.

"We want to talk to somebody about your facility," Sunnie said. "Are you in charge?"

The woman snorted and then yelled over her shoulder, "Hey, Doc! Some people to see you." Turning back to Sandy and Sunnie, she said, "Good luck keeping him awake." Then she hit the swinging half door at the end of the counter with her fist, rushed through it and out the office door.

From the inner office came a short man in an old-fashioned gray suit and round, wire-rimmed glasses. He blinked, smoothed his fringe of white hair, and asked hesitantly, "What can I do to help you?"

"We'd like a tour of Walnut Manor," Sunnie said.

"Really?" the man asked. "It's been years since I've given a tour, but sure, I can do that, I guess. How come you're interested in Walnut Manor?"

"We're looking for a good convalescent hospital for some members of our family."

"Some?" the man asked. "There's more than one?"

"Three," Sunnie said, deliberately neglecting to mention Attila. This would be hard enough to explain without bringing in a chicken.

"Three!" the man said, brightening considerably. "Well. I'm Dr. Waldemar, the director, and we definitely have room for three more." He came around the counter to shake hands with them. He gave them each a brochure and fee schedule.

"Who was that woman?" Sandy asked, unable to restrain his curiosity any longer.

"Oh, that's Opal, our nurse. But please, don't let appearances deceive you; she's highly competent. Living out here in the country, we've both gotten a little out of touch with current fashions. I believe that the quality of the heart that lies beneath the clothes is more important than the clothes themselves."

"Nobody could argue with that," Sandy said.

"I must tell you," Dr. Waldemar said, "that our patient count has been dwindling for some time. For one thing, we're so far from town that it's difficult for families to come visit. And for another, insurance companies don't pay for our services the way they used to, so we can keep only those patients who can personally afford our care. We've had to close off one wing to keep costs down, and we no longer heat the pool. But I assure you," he added hastily, "our guests get the finest care."

"Could we see some of the guests?" Sunnie asked.

"Certainly. They should be in the library now. After breakfast they're supposed to straighten their rooms, and then they spend most of the rest of the day in the library. We keep the fire going, and it's quite cozy."

They crossed the wide central hall to the library's double doors, which Dr. Waldemar opened. The library was a large, elegantly proportioned room, with a coffered ceiling and two walls of bookshelves rising all the way to it. At the far end of the room, French doors opened out onto a stone porch. In the center of the remaining wall, a fireplace blazed away cheerfully.

A pale, potato-shaped man sat on a couch in front of a televised exercise program twitching his arms and shoulders in a pallid imitation of what the instructor on the screen was doing. Another pale, potato-shaped man sat next to him doing nothing.

At a table in the middle of the room, four men were playing cards. One of the men wore a yachting cap; one had a full, white, Santa Claus beard; and one had his thumb in his mouth. Everything about the fourth man could be characterized as "average"; the police would never have been able to identify him from a description of all his average attributes.

A thin young man was lying on a wheeled platform resting next to one of the bookcases, and another young man, who looked to be about seventeen and to weigh close to three hundred pounds, stood at the French doors looking out onto the empty flower beds.

"We're down to eight now," Dr. Waldemar said. "And most of them have been here for a long, long time. I don't know why they're all men. Maybe families are more willing to take care of their distressed female relatives at home. Maybe females don't get as distressed. I just don't know."

As Dr. Waldemar, Sunnie, and Sandy stood inside the door talking, all the men at the card table put down their cards and looked at them.

"We have some visitors today," Dr. Waldemar said. "We'll be on our best behavior, won't we?"

The man with the beard and the man with the yachting cap gave almost identical scowls and picked up their cards.

The average-looking man at the card table said, " 'You can observe a lot just by watching.' Yogi Berra."

Sunnie glanced at Dr. Waldemar.

"That's Everett. He always speaks in quotations. He

doesn't see any reason to speak in his own words because he thinks somebody else has already said it better than he can."

" 'I quote others only the better to express myself.' Michel de Montaigne," Everett said.

"Michel de Montaigne. 1533 to 1592," Sandy said.

Sunnie stared at him. So did Dr. Waldemar and Everett. Then Everett jumped up, ran to Sandy, and embraced him. He drew back and regarded Sandy sternly. " 'Beware of false knowledge,' " he said, " 'it is more dangerous than ignorance.' George Bernard Shaw."

"It's not false," Sandy said, a little indignantly. "My family and I read a lot of Montaigne when I was growing up. Montaigne said something I've been thinking about a lot lately."

"What's that?" Dr. Waldemar asked.

"He said 'What do I know?' " Sandy replied.

Everett embraced Sandy again, with tears in his eyes. " 'One's friends are that part of the human race with which one can be human.' George Santayana."

"Sorry," Sandy said. "I don't know anything about George Santayana."

When Everett had gone back to the card table, Dr. Waldemar led Sunnie and Sandy out into the hall and closed the doors behind them.

"What's wrong with all those people?" Sandy asked.

"Nothing serious, most of them. Just bothersome to their families, really. You heard Everett. All those quotes were driving his wife crazy. And he gets over-excited by anybody else who knows a quote, the way he did with you. The one with the thumb in his mouth, Boom-Boom, now he's an interesting case. He's a split personality, one part grown-up, and the other part still a little child. Switches back and forth all the time. The man with the white beard, that's Whitney Hamilton Atherton Moreland III. Maybe you've heard of him. He's one of the richest men in the country, but he was getting so forgetful, he couldn't run his business anymore. He's so irascible, none of his family would take him in. He's been here for eight or nine years. Let's see. The one with the yachting cap, that's L. Barlow Van Dyke, another rich man. But hard to get along with, too. In fact, the last time he spoke to anybody was the day his family brought him here, about the same time Mr. Moreland arrived. Hasn't said a word since. But he can scowl volumes. The fat boy, Graham, is just too depressed about being fat to go to school anymore. He couldn't take the teasing. His parents won't let him come home until he slims down and cheers up, but he hasn't lost an ounce or smiled since he's been here."

"What about the boy lying down?"

"That's Eddy, our most serious case. One day he just lay down—said he was tired—and he's never gotten up again. Hasn't spoken again, either. He's not much trouble, but I do feel sorry for him, wasting his youth like that. His parents haven't been to see him in ages. The two on the couch, Virgil and Lyle, are bachelor brothers. They just aren't suited for modern life, I think. They're afraid of everything. When it got to the point where they were afraid to leave their house—they lived together—their married sisters shipped them here, where the only life they experience is on TV."

"Are the patients getting any kind of treatment?" Sunnie asked.

"Oh, no," Dr. Waldemar replied. "There's really not much we can do for them. Either they haven't responded to treatment, like Eddy and Boom-Boom, or they're too uncooperative to treat, like L. Barlow Van Dyke and Whitney Hamilton Atherton Moreland III, or they're perfectly satisfied the way they are, like Virgil and Lyle and Everett."

"What about Graham?" Sunnie asked.

"He won't even try. He just mopes and eats. So what we do is keep them comfortable and entertained. To tell you the truth, if any of them were to get better, they wouldn't have any place to go. Their families really don't want them back."

Dr. Waldemar showed Sunnie and Sandy around the rest of Walnut Manor, and everywhere they looked, they saw Opal at work. As they walked through the grounds, she was up in a tree sawing off a broken limb. Then she applied mortar to some bricks that had fallen out of the wall separating Walnut Manor from Eclipse.

Later, in the kitchen, they saw her chopping vegetables and tossing them into a large kettle on the stove. When she finished chopping, she stirred the soup with one hand and spread peanut butter on slices of bread with the other.

Upstairs, she skated down the hall, dust mops on

her feet and a paintbrush in her hand, touching up chips in the wall as she went.

"How big is your staff here?" Sunnie asked Dr. Waldemar.

"Now there's just Opal and me. It's hard to get the kind of help we need, way out here in the country. When it got so we couldn't attract any nurses, Opal took a nursing degree through correspondence school. You never knew when she'd come flying at you to practice her tourniquets or try to change your bed with you still in it."

"How can you get a nursing degree through correspondence school?" Sunnie wondered.

"It ain't easy," Opal replied, skating by on her dust mops.

"We both live on the premises," Dr. Waldemar said as they started down the stairs. "So the patients are never left unattended. Opal grows a vegetable garden in the summer and cans the produce for winter. We're almost self-sustaining. We've got a few chickens for eggs and a cow for milk and butter."

"Thank you for the tour, Dr. Waldemar," Sunnie said. "We'll talk it over and let you know."

"Ah, exactly what is it that *three* members of your family have?" asked Dr. Waldemar as he walked them to the door.

"Comas," Sunnie said, opening the door. "Bye."

Dr. Waldemar's mouth gaped as if to say something, but Sunnie took Sandy's hand and pulled him down the stairs to their bicycles. Dr. Waldemar watched, his mouth still ajar, as they rode away.

As soon as Dr. Waldemar and Walnut Manor were out of sight, Sunnie began to giggle.

"What's so funny?" Sandy asked.

"Oh, Sandy, did you see the look on Dr. Waldemar's face? Do you think for one minute he believed we have three comatose relatives? *Nobody* has *three* comatose relatives. Oh, is he going to be surprised when we move them in there."

"You think we should put them in Walnut Manor?"

"Yes, I do. Maybe something funny's going on there, but it's plain to see Dr. Waldemar and Opal like the patients and treat them well. That's worth a lot more than a heated swimming pool and gourmet meals. Besides, the location can't be beat."

"What do you mean something funny's going on there?" Sandy asked as they pedaled down the road toward Eclipse. "It didn't look like a funny place to me."

"Not that kind of funny. I mean, a place that charges the kind of fees that place does shouldn't have to turn off the heat in the swimming pool and serve peanut butter sandwiches for lunch and keep a cow and chickens. And they should have more staff. And those patients should be getting some kind of treatment, not just sitting around playing cards and watching TV. Oh, what a challenge that place could be. How I'd love an assignment like that. It would be heaven!"

"Sunnie, if we're going to put Horatio and Mousey and Flossie and Attila in Walnut Manor, I want you to go with them. Opal's too busy to give them the care they need. I won't feel right about sending them there unless you say you'll go, too."

Sunnie looked at him. Tears gleamed in her eyes and her bicycle wobbled precariously. "Oh, Sandy, what a lovely thing to say. There's nothing I'd like better. I could hardly bear the idea of leaving Eclipse and . . . and my dear patients. If your lawyers say it's OK, then I'd love to stay. You know, I'm a little like the people at Walnut Manor; if I left here, I don't know where I'd go. I don't have any parents, and now that I'm finished with nursing school, I don't even have a dormitory to live in. And I'd have hated to leave here without knowing how the story ended. The story of your parents, I mean. I want to be around when they wake up. I'll stay right here with them until they're all right, even if it takes years."

"In a way, I hope it does," Sandy murmured, gazing at Sunnie with gratitude, and also with something else—something more complicated and harder to understand.

"You know," Sunnie said, pedaling straight again, "I like to think of life as a story. Somehow that helps it make sense. When something bad is happening, like when my mother died, I think, *If I were making this into a story, what would I have happen next?* And I think up something that helps me get through the bad part. I admit I never would have thought of having my father die at the same time as my mother and leave me money for nursing school, but that turned out to be better than anything I did think up. Do you ever do that?"

"No," admitted Sandy. "But this is the first time anything bad has happened to me."

"Well, how would you like it to end?"

"Of course I want my parents and Flossie and Attila to be all right—"

"Don't worry," she interrupted. "They will be."

"And I want Bart and Bernie to get what they deserve. They were bad enough when all they were was lazy and greedy. But now, since they tried to kill us and then blame me for what happened, they're worse than anything I could have thought up for a story."

"Absolutely right," she said. "What else?"

"You're not going to like this part. I'd like to spend more time in the city. I know you think Eclipse is perfect, but you've known another life. There is so much energy and excitement in the city, something I've never felt, living in Eclipse. I like it."

She thought for a moment, a frown between her perfect eyebrows. "Maybe you need a place like Eclipse to make you appreciate the city. And vice versa. Well, if that's what you want, then that's the way I want your story to go, too."

They parked their bicycles in the front drive of Eclipse and went inside to tell Bentley about Walnut Manor.

10

The day of the move, a parade of ambulances delivered Mousey, Horatio, Flossie, and Attila to Walnut Manor while all the residents except Eddy stood on the broad porch watching. Dr. Waldemar had opened a section of the closed wing for the new patients, and furnished an adjoining bedroom for Sunnie. Sunnie carried Attila, in the dishpan, through the front door. This was the first Dr. Waldemar and the others knew that a chicken was to be one of the patients.

As she passed Graham, Sunnie pointed to him and said, "You're a big strong boy. How about taking my suitcase up to my room?"

Graham shambled forward and grabbed the handle of the suitcase. He pulled it toward him but it didn't budge. He pulled again, harder, and this time it moved a couple of inches. "What have you got in here?" he asked, astonished.

"Books," she said, coming back onto the porch, the dishpan in her arms. "I don't have time right now to explain my theories of education to you, but I can tell you that I believe in continuing to learn, and after a bit of experimenting, I settled on a method of picking a subject and reading in depth on it. I've just finished an extensive study of whales—nothing personal," she said, eyeing Graham's girth. "I figure if I give three months to each subject, that's four a year. In ten years I'll know a lot about forty different things. How many people do you know who know a lot about forty different things? I can see already that some subjects will be more interesting to me than others. Whales weren't too bad, and they did get more interesting as I went along, though I wasn't sure they would at first. I even read a book from the whales' point of view. It was all about what they thought and how they felt and how they communicated with each other. The book said they had ESP. But it seems so far-fetched to me. Like imagining Louie sitting around composing poetry in his head. I *know* he doesn't do that. At least I don't think he does. Oh dear, now I'm all confused. Well, come on, let's get this stuff unloaded so we can get settled in. Some day soon you and I have to have a nice chat." She turned and carried Attila into Walnut Manor.

Graham looked after her, a dazed expression on his round face. "Who's Louie?" he asked. No one on the porch knew, so he wrestled with the suitcase again, finally dragging it up the steps and through the door.

There was a great deal of commotion as people went back and forth, up and down the stairs, carrying things, depositing things, dropping things. Finally the sleepers were settled in their room, Sunnie's suitcase was unpacked, and Sandy and Bentley were sadly contemplating returning to Eclipse alone.

"Oh, you might as well stay for supper," Opal said, looking at their crestfallen expressions. "It's nothing special."

Sunnie decided to eat her dinner on a tray in her patients' room so she could make sure the travel hadn't harmed them, but the others gathered around a single long table in the dining room.

Opal had made a great pot of spaghetti and a big green salad, and as she dished up the plates, she announced that dessert would be canned peaches from Walnut Manor's own trees and anybody who didn't like that could just lump it.

Sandy thought Opal's spaghetti sauce was the best he'd ever tasted, but he didn't say so for fear of hurting Bentley's feelings. Bentley was quite proud of his own spaghetti sauce.

Mr. Moreland leaned across the table toward Sandy and said, "That's a good-looking nurse you've brought along. I seem to remember her from somewhere. What's her name? Stormy? Windy? I can't remember anything anymore."

"Her name's Sunnie." Sandy loved to say her name. "And you saw her a few days ago when we came to take a tour of Walnut Manor."

"Is that so?" Mr. Moreland asked.

Everett nudged Sandy with his elbow. " 'She had curves in places other women don't even have places.' Cybill Shepherd said that about Marilyn Monroe."

"She may be right," Sandy said. "I don't know much about women."

"I must be forgetting what *I* knew about them," Mr. Moreland said. "Today I pinched Opal. She almost broke my arm after I did it."

" 'Happiness? That's nothing more than health and a poor memory.' Albert Schweitzer," Everett said.

"What a bunch of balderdash," Mr. Moreland retorted grumpily. "I've got them both and they don't add up to happiness. I used to be able to hold a full day's quotes from the Big Board in my head, and now I can hardly remember the difference between stocks and bonds. There was a time L. Barlow Van Dyke and I were making money so fast we didn't have time to count it. We were young, stubborn, ambitious, competitive. I beat him by one week to making my first million, but he made his second before I did. After that, we quit counting. Now look at us. I can hardly remember my own name, and he sits around looking like a thundercloud. Who'd ever have thought we'd end up like this? Last time I saw him out in the world he was making a speech at some big function, and now he's not only mute, he's a cat molester."

"A cat molester?" Bentley asked, alarmed, raising his voice slightly to be heard over the sound of Graham's chewing. Graham was already on thirds, while everyone else was still on firsts. "You mean he teases cats? Manhandles them? Torments, harasses, badgers, and annoys them?" Bentley had spent many hours reading the thesaurus.

"I suppose. That's the last thing he said the day he checked in here. Opal asked him what we should call him, and he said, 'Cat molester,' and he's never said another word. I guess he's ashamed of how far he's fallen."

There was a little commotion at the other end of the table where Boom-Boom sat. He had spilled his milk and now was scolding himself while his other half cried. Opal got up for a sponge and cleaned up the milk before she went back to taking one bite for herself and then giving one bite to Eddy who lay on his padded, wheeled platform next to her chair.

After dinner, which Sandy had enjoyed immensely, he and Bentley went upstairs to say good night to Sunnie and the sleepers.

As Sandy and Bentley drove back to Eclipse in the dark, Sandy sighed and said, "It doesn't feel right, just the two of us going home. Two's not enough. I want Horatio and Mousey and Flossie and Attila back." He was afraid to say he wanted Sunnie back—afraid Bentley would hear the longing in his voice. "I wish there was something we could do."

"I've been reading up, and I'm going to try something," Bentley said. "Remember our chemistry experiments in the kitchen?"

"Sure. You discovered that formula to make plastic from potato peels."

"Right. Well, I'm going back to experimenting. To see if I can find a cure."

"But Bentley, you don't know anything about medicine. This could be dangerous."

"I know a lot more about medicine now than I did a couple of months ago. I'll test my experiments on Attila."

"What if they don't work?"

"I'll just keep trying until I find something that does."

"I mean, what if . . ."

"I know what you mean. I'll have to be careful."

Bentley pulled the Daimler into the garage.

"Please be *very* careful," Sandy said.

The next morning, after breakfast, Bentley drove Sandy to Walnut Manor. After he visited Flossie, Bentley went home to begin his experiments, leaving Sandy at Walnut Manor until supper time.

"Now, Sandy," Sunnie told him after they'd finished the morning chores for their patients, "my new field of study is finance, and it's as much for your benefit as for mine. If you ever want to get control of your father's money and secure it against Bart and Bernie, you've got to educate yourself. You've got to learn about buying on margin, and tax shelters, and depreciation, and things like that."

"What?" She might have been speaking a foreign language to him.

"That's all part of a sound financial education, Sandy, and you have to start now."

"Oh, all right. If you say so. But it sounds so difficult and dull."

"Well, it sounds difficult to me, too. After all, I don't know much more than you. But I do know about checking accounts and income tax. I still have trouble reconciling my bank statement, but at least I know how it's supposed to be done. Somebody told me not to bother because the bank is never wrong and I should just trust the amount on the statement, but I discovered once that the computer had stuttered or something. Instead of subtracting a check for $8.79, it subtracted $888.79, so it does pay to be alert. And if that kind of mistake could happen in a little checking account like mine, why, just think of what could go wrong with a financial empire like your father's."

"I'm sure my father has accountants or something to handle things like that. They'd spot it."

"They could be embezzlers. Now sit down and let me read this book to you. It's called *Earning, Spending, Saving, Investing, Borrowing, and Losing.*"

Before Sandy could get to a chair, Opal appeared in the doorway and said, "I need another pair of hands. You aren't doing anything that shows to the naked eye. Come on." She grabbed him by the arm and pulled him out of the room.

Sunnie watched him go, then shrugged and opened her book.

"It's cold in the library," Opal said, dragging Sandy down the stairs, "and I can't light another fire until all the old ashes have been cleaned out of the fireplace. Dr. Waldemar's taking a nap, and I've got to get lunch going. You're elected." She towed him into the library and left him staring forlornly into the cold fireplace, which brimmed with ashes.

Behind him Mr. Moreland, L. Barlow Van Dyke, Boom-Boom, and Everett sat at the card table, in coats and gloves, playing their usual game. Virgil and Lyle sat on the couch, a blanket wrapped around them, watching television. They had a schedule they abided by, watching the same programs every day. The only conflict they had was at 11:00 A.M., when Virgil wanted to watch *Bowling for Dollars* and Lyle wanted to watch *I Love Lucy* reruns. They compromised, alternating days for those programs.

"Hurry up and get that fireplace ready," Mr. Moreland said. "I'm freezing."

"And it's harder to cheat when you're dealing the cards with gloves on," Boom-Boom said in his little kid's voice. "Boom-Boom," he said in his grown-up voice, "that isn't very nice. Now apologize to Mr. Moreland." "No," he answered, sticking his thumb in his mouth.

Sandy tentatively took a shovelful of ashes from the fireplace and deposited it in a brown paper grocery sack. A fine gray cloud rose from it and floated over the hearth, settling slowly onto the carpet and making Sandy cough.

Graham turned from the windows, where he was looking out onto a barren winter landscape. "Why don't you wet the ashes down before you shovel them? Then they won't fly around like that."

"That's a great idea," Sandy said with admiration. Graham flushed and turned back to the window as Sandy went off to the kitchen to get a pitcher of water.

Working at the messy job, he listened to the sounds of the TV and the four men playing cards, and he was glad they'd decided to put Mousey and Horatio and Flossie and Attila here.

"Well, LBVD," Mr. Moreland said, slapping his cards on the table, "that makes two million, three hundred and fifty-seven thousand, nineteen dollars and twenty-four cents you owe me." He scraped together the cards from the other players and shuffled them. L. Barlow Van Dyke scowled more darkly than usual and stuck his gloved hands in his pockets.

" 'That money talks/I'll not deny,/I heard it once:/It said, "Goodbye." ' Richard Armour," Everett said.

"Not to me, it doesn't," Mr. Moreland said. "I know more about earning, spending, saving, investing, and borrowing money than any man alive." He sighed. "At least, I used to."

"You don't seem to have forgotten anything about playing cards," Sandy said. "It sounds like you've won a lot of money playing them."

"True. But I didn't learn to play until I got to Walnut Manor. I never had time before. It's the things I did out *there*," he gestured in the direction of the windows, "that I have trouble remembering."

Sandy put the last shovelful of ashes into the grocery sack. He had just finished laying the new fire when Sunnie came into the library. "Sandy, why don't you go sit with your family? I know you'd like to spend some time with them, and I'd like to get to know these gentlemen, since it looks as if we're going to be spending a lot of time together. Go on. I'll light the fire."

Sandy left the room, and Sunnie touched a match to the fire starter amid the logs in the fireplace. Then she pulled a chair up to the card table and sat down. "Go ahead," she said. "Don't mind me. I just want to watch. I'm not much at cards, unless you count Go Fish and Old Maid. I used to play them by the hour with my mother while she sat at the window watching for my father. Evenings were especially hard for her and she needed distractions. I've found that most people have one time of day that's most difficult for them. It was dusk for my mother. All that blue light, maybe. For some people it's early morning. Hard starters, I call them. One of my patients in nurses' training hated 2:30 in the afternoon. She said everything bad that had ever happened to her happened at 2:30 in the afternoon. She'd had a car crash at 2:30, lost a job at 2:30, been left standing at the altar at 2:30. She'd even broken her leg skiing at 2:30. That's what she was in the hospital for, a broken leg. I suggested maybe she could have her watch fixed so it would go straight from 2:29 to 2:31 without stopping at 2:30, the way some hotels have elevators that go from the twelfth floor to the fourteenth floor with no thirteenth floor in between. Of course, there *is* a thirteenth floor, they're just calling it by another name, so I don't know who they're trying to kid."

As Sunnie talked, Boom-Boom edged his chair closer to hers, stuck his thumb in his mouth, and leaned his head on her shoulder. She glanced down at him, smiled, and kept talking.

"I suppose it would mess up her time, eventually. She'd be a minute short every day so—let me see—in two months she'd be an hour late for everything. Or would it be an hour early? Anyway, she'd be an hour off, and in a year that would be six hours. That's a lot—"

"Bicuspid!" Mr. Moreland exploded. "I can't hear myself think. How do you expect me to deal a hand of cards when I can't concentrate?"

"Oh, I'm sorry," Sunnie said. "Sometimes I get going and I can't find a good stopping place. Why did you say 'bicuspid'?"

"Opal won't let me cuss. She says it lowers the tone of the place. But there're times I *need* to cuss, so I have to use other words that sound like cussing."

Everett smiled at Sunnie. "He is 'the most even-tempered man I ever knew. Always mad.' Attributed to a friend of Pancho Gonzales."

"Oh, he doesn't scare me," Sunnie said. "There's nothing wrong with him a good megadose of B-complex vitamins wouldn't cure."

"For your information, young lady," Mr. Moreland said, "my memory is shot full of holes. You can't plug them with vitamin pills."

"Would you be willing to give it a try?" Sunnie asked.

"Won't do any good," he said.

"I'll bring you some to take with your lunch," she said, gently lifting Boom-Boom's head from her shoulder. "You can get on with your game. I'll go sit with Virgil and Lyle."

Boom-Boom sucked his thumb and looked longingly after her as she walked across the room.

"Schnauzer!" Mr. Moreland cussed. "She may have curves in places other girls don't even have places, but she hasn't got much between the ears."

Sunnie turned and smiled at him before she sat down on the couch with Lyle and Virgil, the pale, potato-shaped TV watchers. They both looked quickly at her out of the corners of their eyes and hastily turned back to the TV screen. They were as afraid of her as they were of everything else.

"What are these patches on your jackets?" Sunnie asked, pointing to two emblems on Virgil's jacket. Lyle's jacket was identical to Virgil's.

Virgil mumbled something.

"What?" Sunnie asked. "I can't hear you."

Virgil mumbled a little louder. Sunnie looked questioningly at him and then at Lyle.

"He's shy," Lyle whispered. "I've always been the bold one." He blushed and looked at his shoes. "The patches are from two clubs we belong to." His voice dwindled away to nothing.

"What clubs?" Sunnie asked. "This looks like a picture of a potato on a couch."

Lyle glanced quickly up at her and then down at his shoes again. "It is," he whispered. "We're Couch Potatoes."

"Couch potatoes?"

"Yes. It's an organization of people who watch a lot of television. The other patch is from the Flat Earth Society."

"But the earth is round," Sunnie said.

"Oh, no," Virgil said, speaking intelligibly for the first time. "Anybody can see the edge."

"But that's an illusion," Sunnie said. "There's lots more past the horizon."

Virgil and Lyle stared at their shoes and shook their heads back and forth like the pendulum on a clock.

"Oh, well," Sunnie said. "Tell me about the Couch Potatoes."

"You can join," Lyle whispered. "The ladies' group is the Couch Tomatoes. The children are Tater Tots."

"That's sweet of you," Sunnie said, "but I don't watch much TV. I'd rather read. I'd be glad to loan you some books. I have lots."

"TV's easier," Virgil whispered.

"Didn't anybody ever read to you while you were growing up?" Sunnie asked.

"Big family. No time," Lyle replied.

"Well, you've missed a lot of good books. I'm going to ask Opal if I can read aloud after dinner. Would you like that? We can make popcorn and sit here in front of the fire. I love to read out loud. I used to read to my mother all the time, especially when she was sick. Mostly, I read to her from my schoolbooks so I could kill two birds . . . well, that's not a very nice way to put it, is it? I don't think my reading had anything to do with my mother's death, but she certainly died well informed. I hope she can use all that American history and algebra wherever she is now. To tell you the truth, I haven't found much use for it where I've been since then, but it must be some good or they wouldn't teach it so much in school, right? Well, you get back to your TV while I go talk to Opal."

Sunnie stood up and bumped into Graham, who had gradually edged closer and closer to the conversation from his usual post by the windows. "I'm sorry, Graham. Did you want something?"

"Would you read *The Wind in the Willows*? I have a copy."

"Of course. Is that a favorite book of yours?"

"Oh, yes. Especially the picnic where Mole and Ratty take 'coldchickencoldtonguecoldhamcoldbeef-pickledgherkinssaladfrenchrollscresssandwidgespotted-meatgingerbeerlemonadesodawater—' "

"Yes, yes," Sunnie said. "I have to go talk to Opal. I'll expect to see you here after dinner tonight."

After dinner, to which Bentley and Sandy were again invited, Dr. Waldemar went upstairs to sit with the sleepers, and Sunnie took Graham's *The Wind in the Willows* into the library, where she sat in a chair before the fire and began to read. Boom-Boom sprawled on the floor at her feet, and Eddy's platform was rolled up near her. The others pulled chairs around her, except for Virgil and Lyle, who cooperated by turning the TV lower so it wouldn't interfere with the reading. L. Barlow Van Dyke and Mr. Moreland sat somewhat farther back, with their arms crossed over their chests.

When Sunnie finished the first chapter, she raised her head and was pleasantly surprised to find herself surrounded by a ring of spellbound faces, including Mr. Moreland's and Mr. Van Dyke's. Virgil and Lyle, for once, were turned away from the TV set. Boom-Boom leaned his head against her knee. "Read some more," he said, and put his thumb in his mouth. All the heads nodded in agreement.

The room was in darkness except for the fire, one lamp on the table at Sunnie's elbow, and the blue glow of the TV. Sunnie turned back to her book and read the next chapter, in which Toad wrecks his beautiful gypsy wagon and falls in love with motorcars.

Sandy sat back in his chair, barely listening. He'd read *The Wind in the Willows* so often he'd almost memorized it. So he let the smooth sound of Sunnie's voice flow around him like water, carrying off some of the day's cares.

"Now, my friends," Sunnie said at the end of the chapter. "I'll have to stop if you want me to have any voice left for reading tomorrow. Besides, look how late it is. I must check on my patients. But tell me, didn't you enjoy that? And there are so many more wonderful books to read. Tonight you can all dream about traveling in a beautiful yellow gypsy cart like Toad's or rowing down the river for a picnic with Mole and Ratty. Let your imaginations take you on a trip. I'll bet none of you have given much thought to what it would be like to live in a hole by a riverbank, have you?"

In a thoughtful silence the inmates of Walnut Manor drifted out of the library to their rooms. Sandy knew he should get ready to leave, but he dreaded going back to poor Eclipse, so cold and empty now with everyone but Bentley gone all day. While Sunnie was reading, he had felt part of a big family. He sighed and went upstairs with Sunnie and Bentley to say good night to the sleepers.

"Sandy," Sunnie said. "I think it would be nice if you brought Louie over tomorrow. I'm sure he misses Attila and, who knows, maybe Attila misses him, too."

"What about L. Barlow Van Dyke, the cat molester? What if he tries to hurt Louie?"

"We'll look after Louie," she said. "Bring him tomorrow."

"Well, all right," he said. "If you think it's okay."

On their way back to Eclipse, Sandy asked Bentley how his experiments had gone that day.

"Nothing to shout about yet," Bentley said, "although I might be on to something promising. It'll take a few days. But I did devise a signal bell we can attach to each of the sleepers. If something about their conditions changes, the bell rings. That way, someone doesn't have to be with them all the time. Like tonight. While Sunnie was reading, Dr. Waldemar had to be sitting upstairs. If we have a warning bell, Sunnie can have a little more freedom."

"That's a good idea. I know this sounds strange, Bentley, but I love being at Walnut Manor. All the people are so interesting and there's always something going on."

"Maybe living out here so isolated for such a long time wasn't a very good idea," Bentley said. "Your mother and father were both tired of the city and all its problems, and so were Flossie and I; but maybe we should have balanced things better for you."

"Oh, I've loved living at Eclipse," Sandy assured Bentley. "But I am getting curious about what else there is. Bentley, would you teach me to drive?"

"Sure, I'll teach you to drive," Bentley said, even though he knew that once someone knew how to drive, the next thing he'd want would be to go somewhere.

CHAPTER

11

- - - - - - -

The next day Sandy drove the Daimler jerkily around and around the circular driveway, popping the clutch and leaving black tire marks behind him, while Bentley sucked in his breath and wished there were a brake pedal on the floor of the passenger's side of the car.

"There's more to this than I thought," Sandy said. "Bentley, you make it look so easy."

When they arrived at Walnut Manor, with Bentley gratefully behind the wheel of the Daimler, Sandy tucked Louie under his coat when he got out of the car. He looked carefully around for L. Barlow Van Dyke before he hurried up the stairs to the sickroom. When he entered the room, making sure the door was solidly closed behind him, Sandy opened his coat, and Louie jumped into Attila's dishpan. He sniffed her face, patted her with his paw, and then snuggled next to her for a nap.

"See?" Sunnie said. "I told you he missed her."

"Just keep L. Barlow out of here." Sandy said good morning to the sleepers, touched their hands and kissed their cheeks, and then said proudly to Sunnie, "I had a driving lesson this morning. It's harder than it looks."

"Well, you're ahead of me there," she said. "I never learned to drive. We couldn't afford a car, so I took the bus and the subway when I wanted to go anywhere. When you learn, will you teach me? Mostly, I believe you can learn anything you need to know from a book, but maybe not driving. And cooking. I'm not sure about that, either. I'm not much of a cook. I was always too busy. I'm a great thawer, though, and a pretty good can opener. I don't know how Opal does it. Three meals a day for all these people, and she never seems to get tired. I wonder if she takes vitamins. I started Mr. Moreland on vitamins yesterday. He's skeptical, but I'm not. I've seen what vitamins can do—with depressed people and alcoholics and all kinds of problems. Just you wait and see. In a couple of weeks, his memory will start to improve and he'll be feeling ever so much better. Part of the reason he's as irritable as he is, is because he's scared. Think how you'd feel if you couldn't trust your own mind and you'd forgotten a lot of the things that made you important. There's nothing wrong with Mr. Moreland except that nobody wants him. Same with most of these people. Boom-Boom needs a mother. I don't know what kind of a mother he had to start with, but there's a part of him that didn't get enough mothering and it won't grow up until it gets some more. Graham needs to feel important. He's so fat because he's comforting himself with food. What kind of parents would put a nice young man like Graham in a place like this just because he eats too much? And poor little Virgil and Lyle. They're just afraid to live, and probably always have been, from the sound of things. Imagine believing the earth is flat! Why, if they'd ever taken a trip anywhere they'd know you don't fall off the edge. Sandy, once you've taught me, I'm going to take them for a long drive right over the edge of the horizon and *show* them. It's such a beautiful big world out there—parts of it, anyway. I *will not* let them sit indoors watching television forever. You only get one life. Everett, he's okay. He must be very educated and well read to know so many quotes. And he's got a point. Somebody else usually *has* said it better. I can see where his habit annoyed his wife, but nothing's wrong with him. And I'm going to get L. Barlow to talk, if it kills me. Now Eddy, he has me worried. He's not like the rest. He doesn't do *anything*. Why is that? Oh, Sandy, this is just a dream come true for me. All these wonderful patients to take care of. A nice place to live. And time to read. I thank my lucky stars every day for sending me to Eclipse."

"I thank mine, too." Sandy said. "For sending you."

"I do my best," she said modestly. "Now, Sandy, you run along. I have to bathe my patients and do my morning chores. I'll see you at lunch."

Sandy went downstairs, where he was invited to join the card game.

"I played a lot of cards with my parents when I was younger, but I don't know if I can keep up with you."

"Sit down and give it a try," Mr. Moreland said, anticipating having someone new to beat.

So Sandy joined the game and surprised himself by winning almost every hand. Everybody else was surprised, too. Boom-Boom stuck his thumb in his mouth and sulked and refused to pick up his cards when they were dealt to him. He told himself that nobody likes a poor loser, but he didn't listen.

Mr. Moreland, dismayed at losing for the first time in years, began to criticize Sandy's card-playing strategy as disorganized, haphazard, and just phenomenally lucky. He went on so long that Boom-Boom got bored and wandered over to watch a bit of TV with Virgil and Lyle before lunch. L. Barlow Van Dyke glowered and shuffled the cards over and over, and Everett pulled a book out of his pocket and began reading it.

"I never realized playing cards could be so complicated," Sandy said. "I thought games were for fun."

"Winning's the fun part," Mr. Moreland said. "Even if you just do it by luck. But I can tell that even somebody who plays like you do has a natural ability for management," he finally conceded.

Everett raised his head from his book and remarked, " 'Life is like a game of cards. The hand that is dealt you represents determinism; the way you play it is free will.' Jawaharlal Nehru."

"Look how much you've learned from me already about playing cards," Mr Moreland said, forgetting that Sandy had beaten him *before* his directions. "If I still had my wits, I could teach you lots of things. Why, I could teach you so much about managing money you'd be a millionaire in a year."

"I think I already am a millionaire."

"Inherited money doesn't count," Mr. Moreland sniffed. "You don't have the passion for it that you do for the stuff you make by yourself. You should have that pleasure, boy."

"It's too bad you can't teach me. Sunnie wants me to learn about finance, but the book is so thick and the print is so small, I don't even want to start."

"You have to have your hands on money to make finance interesting, boy. Dealing with it theoretically out of a book won't work. I think maybe we should play some Monopoly instead of cards. L. Barlow would like that, too. He was always a nut for making money." He sighed. "Now he's just a nut. Like the rest of us."

"Sunnie doesn't think you're nuts," Sandy said. "Just—I don't know—misunderstood? Unappreciated? Something like that."

"Oh, what does she know?" Mr. Moreland asked grumpily. "She's just a kid."

Sandy, who had thought Mr. Moreland would be pleased that someone thought he wasn't a nut, was puzzled. Was Mr. Moreland just so contrary that he automatically disagreed with everything, or was his re-action something Sandy would have understood if he'd been more worldly? A few months ago he'd thought he knew everything worth knowing, but lately he'd realized how much more complicated real life was than the safe, simple imitation of it he'd had at Eclipse.

CHAPTER

12

Fortunately there was little traffic on Old Country Road. Sandy was now driving the Daimler from Eclipse to Walnut Manor every morning, while Bentley sat beside him holding his breath and pressing his right foot into the floor.

After a quick visit to see his parents, Flossie, Attila, and Louie (who stayed at Walnut Manor all the time now but wasn't allowed to leave the sickroom for fear of L. Barlow Van Dyke, the cat molester), Sandy always had a visit with Sunnie. Usually she read to him, something he could hardly listen to because he was so absorbed in watching her rosy lips forming the words. And she talked to him, telling him stories of her life, sharing bits from her readings, expressing her opinions on all manner of things. And asking him his.

Sandy was dismayed at the number of times he had to say "I don't know" when she asked him what he thought. He was beginning to wonder if, for all his educational advantages, he actually ever *had* thought.

After his engrossing, and often bewildering, time with Sunnie, he would go down to the library and play Monopoly with Mr. Moreland and L. Barlow Van Dyke. Boom-Boom and Everett, who weren't interested in finance, played gin rummy games at another table.

L. Barlow Van Dyke had initiated some changes in the Monopoly game that gave them investment options beyond the usual hotels, houses, and railroads: He had made cards allowing them to buy and sell treasury bonds, gold, art, raw land, and pork belly futures.

"Pork belly futures?" Sandy asked, laughing, sure that they were playing a joke on him.

"Don't ever laugh about money," Mr. Moreland said severely. "Pork belly futures are as good a way to increase capital as anything."

"Yes, sir," Sandy said, contrite. It seemed as if every day he discovered a new way in which he was ignorant.

Just before lunch Sunnie would come downstairs, knowing that if anything changed with her patients, she would hear the bell Bentley had rigged to each of them. She'd put Mr. Moreland's vitamin pills and a glass of water next to the Monopoly board and move on before she had to listen to any of his imaginative cussing.

Sometimes she sat with Virgil and Lyle, watching TV. She made them watch a few minutes a day of TV programs about the outside world: nature, travel, adventure programs.

"Oh, please, Sunnie," they'd beg, agitated and fearful. "Turn back to *Bowling for Dollars*. This program is so . . . so . . ." They never could say exactly what bothered them so much, but, clearly, they suffered. Sunnie tried only once to get them to watch the news. It took them several days, huddling together in front of *Leave It to Beaver* reruns, to recover.

Sometimes she sat on a stool beside Eddy, talking to him about Louie or something she'd read or her mother the actress or her father the street juggler—the same sorts of things she talked to Sandy about each morning. Eddy never responded.

But maybe the way he watched her, rapt and silent, was a response. Sandy thought that he himself must look that way when she talked to him. How he wanted to dazzle her the way she dazzled him, but he knew it was impossible. She must regard him as a child, a simpleton, a boob, the way he was coming to regard himself as he realized more and more how little he knew. Pork belly futures were the least of it.

Sometimes Sunnie played games with Boom-Boom and praised him so lavishly that he smiled shyly around the thumb in his mouth and looked at her adoringly.

While she was engaged in these activities, Mr. Moreland would toss down the handful of vitamins she'd left him and scowl his fanciest scowl at anyone who saw him do it, muttering, "Flotsam! Shinsplints!"

Just before Opal came to call them to lunch, Sunnie sat on the arm of Sandy's chair as he bent over the

Monopoly board, and he felt as if another light had been turned on in the room. Impetuously he gambled a chunk of his money on a long shot, an upstart biotechnology stock bought on margin, flaunting his new expertise like a twelve-year-old showing off on his bike.

13

Competition was always keen as to who would get to sit next to Sunnie at the lunch table. On this day Graham and Dr. Waldemar won.

Opal skated in from the kitchen on her dust mops, with a tureen of soup in her hands and an unlit cigarette in her mouth—she had reluctantly agreed with Sunnie that it was unsafe for her to smoke with oxygen tanks for the sleepers stored upstairs—then skated back to the kitchen for a platter of toasted cheese sandwiches. Outside the big windows, snow fell softly, covering the shuffleboard court and filling the empty pool.

"I used to hate the snow when I was a little girl," Sunnie said, "because my mother was always out in it and I worried about her." She put a sandwich on her plate and one on Graham's, then gently took his hand and shook her head when he reached for another one. "But here it's so beautiful and peaceful, I feel completely different about it. Isn't it funny how I can change my mind like that? Do you know, I've never built a snowman? Have any of you? I know just how to do it. I've read all about it." She grabbed Graham's hand again as he made another attempt at getting an extra sandwich. "I know! We'll make one this afternoon, after I've tended to my sleepers. Yes, all of us; don't you look at each other that way, Virgil and Lyle. It's not as if I'm suggesting anything that will hurt you. It'll be fun, you'll see. Doing it yourself is better than watching someone else do it on TV. Stop scowling at me, Mr. Moreland and Mr. Van Dyke. I'll bet you can make wonderful snowmen. I think you should make snow tycoons and let them light their pipes with dollar bills." She stopped Graham's hand again and gave him a handful of carrot sticks from the relish tray instead. "It's important to keep moving. It always cheers you up to get some exercise."

Suddenly the front door burst open, and Sandy, looking through the big, open dining-room doors and across the wide front hall, saw Bart and Bernie come in, beating the snow off their overcoats and leaving puddles on Opal's polished floor.

"Ah," Bart said, starting across the hall with Bernie trailing him. "Dr. Waldemar?" He held his hand out to Mr. Moreland, who just looked at it.

"I'm Dr. Waldemar," said the genuine article, standing up. "What can I do for you?"

"I'm Bartholemew Huntington and this is my brother Bernard Ackerman. Our brother and sister-in-law, Horatio and Mousey Huntington-Ackerman, are patients here, and we've come to visit them."

"No!" Sandy shouted, jumping to his feet.

Every face at the table turned to Sandy. How could he deny his father and mother visitors? The rest of the inmates would love to have a visitor.

"Don't let them anywhere near Mousey and Horatio. Flossie or Attila, either," Sandy said, coming around the table to stand almost nose to nose with Bart. His heart was pounding so hard he was almost sick— it was a way he'd never felt before in his life—but he would not let Bart and Bernie have another chance to hurt anybody he loved.

"You can't keep us from seeing our own brother," Bart snarled.

"That's what you think," Sandy snarled back, surprised that he knew how to snarl, since he'd never done it before.

Dr. Waldemar looked helplessly from one to the other of them until Opal came skating out of the kitchen with a tray of dishes filled with rice pudding. She deposited her tray on the table and inserted herself between Sandy and Bart. Her cigarette poked Bart in the chin, and he took a step backward.

"What's going on here?" Opal asked. "Who the heck are you two grizzly bears?"

"I'm Mr. Horatio Alger Huntington-Ackerman's brother, and this"—he jerked his thumb at Bernie—"is his other brother. We've come to visit."

"No visitors," Opal said.

"What are you talking about?" Bart snarled again. "He's my brother."

"No visitors. That's our policy with comatose patients," she said. "They're too delicate. Now beat it before I call the cops."

"I can get a court order to see them," Bart said. "I've done it before."

"Goody for you," Opal told him, jabbing him in the chest with her cigarette, which broke in two, half of it sticking to his damp overcoat.

Bernie had already retreated to the front door, but Bart plucked off the broken cigarette, dropped it on the floor, crushed it with his foot, and kept glaring at her. She glared back.

"We'll see about that," Bart said finally, and stalked to the door, slamming it behind him as he left.

A ring of shocked faces around the lunch table looked at Sandy. Opal asked the question they all wanted the answer to: "How come you're so dead set against your uncles seeing your parents?"

"Don't call them my uncles," Sandy said. "I don't want to be related to them in any way. They're attempted murderers."

A gasp went around the table, but not from Opal. She picked up the broken cigarette, rubbed her dust-mopped foot on the spot it left on the floor, and said, "Yeah? Who'd they attempt?"

"Mousey and Horatio and Flossie. I'm afraid I attempted Attila," Sandy said sadly, "but I didn't know the cake was poisoned when I gave it to her."

"Huh?" Opal said, and so did everyone else at the table.

So Sandy sat down and told them the whole story.

When he'd finished, Opal put another unlit cigarette in her mouth and said, "We're going to have some more trouble with them. We'd better be prepared. Hey, Dr. Waldemar, wake up. We've got a problem here."

Dr. Waldemar's chin rested on his chest and his breathing was heavy and regular.

"Shoot," Opal said. "The guy's really slipping. Sometimes I think I ought to park him in an armchair in the library and run the place myself. Which I'm practically doing anyhow." She deposited her cigarette in a cup of rice pudding. "Well, OK. I believe you, kid. We've got to protect our sleepers. Too bad the fancy security system we used to have broke and we never fixed it. Any other suggestions?"

Lyle and Virgil put their arms around each other and shivered. Graham took another rice pudding from the tray and started in on it, first making sure that Sunnie wasn't paying attention. Eddy, of course, didn't do anything, and Boom-Boom sucked furiously on his thumb. Mr. Moreland and Mr. Van Dyke looked at each other, frowning impressively in silent competition, to see who could come up with a suggestion.

"We could hide them," Mr. Moreland said.

L. Barlow Van Dyke made a strangling sound and shook his head.

"Where?" Opal asked. "And what about all their gear?"

"You've got a lot of buildings here, cottages and stables and stuff. Put them in one of those."

L. Barlow Van Dyke's face was turning purple as he shook his head over and over.

"Don't you think a court order would allow Bart and Bernie to search the outbuildings?" Sunnie asked.

L. Barlow Van Dyke paled by a couple of shades and nodded smugly.

"Oh, onion juice!" Mr. Moreland said. "I forgot about that."

"We could say they had something contagious," Sandy suggested. "Then Bart and Bernie couldn't go near them."

Sunnie threw her arms around him. "That's a wonderful idea. Bentley's so clever with his chemistry things. He could cook up something, I'm sure, to make them look sick. Or we could paint spots on them or something. That would keep Bart and Bernie away from them. But it's more important than ever that we get them to wake up. I have an idea of my own," she said, letting go of Sandy. "I think we should all spend more time up there with them. We have to bring them back into life, not keep them isolated. There's a fireplace in their room—I think we should have our after-dinner reading upstairs instead of in the library. Aren't you all tired of sitting around the library, anyway?"

"Is there a TV?" Lyle asked, still clinging to Virgil.

"No," Sunnie said. "Just real people. We'll start tonight, after we've had an afternoon out in the snow. You know, your unconscious works on a problem even when you're doing something else, so while we build our snow people we must all think about keeping our sleepers safe, and who knows what we'll come up with. Now let's go outside."

Every head except Sandy's and Boom-Boom's was shaking from side to side, reluctance as thick in the air as Opal's cigarette smoke used to be. Graham took two more rice puddings from the tray.

"No objections," Sunnie said sternly, returning Graham's puddings to the tray before he could take even one bite. "We're all going outside if I have to dress you up myself. You've got twenty minutes to get ready."

"I want to go out," Boom-Boom said around his thumb.

"Good," Sunnie said. "That shows how smart you are. You know what's good for you."

Boom-Boom beamed.

It was more like an hour before Sunnie got everyone, including Dr. Waldemar, bundled up and out the door to the backyard, but she did it. She herded them ahead of her like a flock of recalcitrant sheep, with Sandy and Boom-Boom as the enthusiastic sheepdogs, pulling Eddy's cart and keeping everyone else in line.

Dr. Waldemar, after messing around with a pile of snow for a few minutes, decided it was too cold for him and went inside. Lyle and Virgil tried to follow him, and so did L. Barlow Van Dyke and Mr. Moreland. But Sunnie stopped them. She said Dr. Waldemar was the boss and the oldest—heavens, he must be eighty—and so he had special privileges. The four men turned around but not without grumbling, at least from three of them. Mr. Van Dyke contributed a virtuoso scowl.

An hour later the yard was populated with a crowd of snow people. Mr. Van Dyke and Mr. Moreland had made two rotund snow tycoons facing each other, their round tummies touching. They each smoked a corncob pipe—goodness only knew where Opal had found them—stuffed with Monopoly money. Lyle and Virgil made identical snowmen, so close together it was impossible to tell where one left off and the other began. Boom-Boom's creation was a snow woman with a snow child tucked into her side. All of Graham's snowmen were slender—with wide shoulders—wonderfully sculpted, and hardened into ice with water he'd brought in a pitcher from the kitchen. Sunnie and Opal between them made a throng of people, in a multitude of shapes, sizes, and genders. Sunnie even made a few four-footed snow creatures of pet size. Opal's figures tended to be less rounded than Sunnie's, but they definitely had energy and originality. She stuck cigarettes in all her snow people's mouths, and Sunnie went around taking them out. Everett didn't make any snow people of his own, but he helped everyone else with theirs. Poor Eddy didn't do anything, of course, but he made an attentive audience, which every performer needs.

Sandy horrified himself by making two snowmen in the shapes of Bart and Bernie—which wasn't hard, because Bart and Bernie were shaped just like snowmen—and then knocking their heads off. As angry as he was, he was ashamed to lower himself to the point where he was acting like they did. He put heads back on his snowmen, but before he knew what he was do-ing, he had knocked them off again. It felt wonderful, he realized with guilty glee. He did it a few more times before he was satisfied to put the heads back on and let them stay.

His life at Eclipse had been so placid, so tranquil that the strongest negative emotions he had ever felt had been annoyance when he couldn't get the top off a jar of pickles and mild irritation at the prospect of having Bart and Bernie for dinner once a month. In the past few weeks, he had discovered an entire catalog of feel-ings he hadn't even known existed: terror at the thought that Horatio, Mousey, Flossie, and Attila might . . . he couldn't even *think* the word; fury and hatred toward Bart and Bernie, plus a real fear that they might try something on Sandy himself; soaring joy at the new things he was learning to do—drive, understand high finance, beat Mr. Moreland at cards without feeling guilty about it. The way Sunnie made him feel occupied a whole category all by itself. Knowing she regarded him with the same fondness she felt for everyone else at Walnut Manor filled him with a sadness that was new to him, too.

He sighed and punched his snowmen in the stom-achs, leaving fist-shaped holes.

"You've made the buttonholes too big," Sunnie said, coming up behind him. "They should be just big enough for a piece of coal. Of course, we don't have any coal, but I think the barbecue briquettes look nice, so square and all. You want some? I'll help you fix the holes in your snowmen." She set to work fixing. "Isn't this fun? Look at all the people we've made. Wouldn't it be perfect if we could make a world exactly the way we want it, with just the people we want in it, the way we've done here? Then there wouldn't be any horrible conflicts and everybody would be happy." She sighed. "Sure, I know there's always conflict, even between people who love each other. But I look at that as good conflict. It's what you have to do to get problems worked out. You can't agree all the time, even with people you love. Think how boring that would be."

That's how it had been at Eclipse, Sandy thought. There was no conflict. And they'd all been happy, hadn't they? But Eclipse, from what he could tell, had almost no relation at all to the real world. Had he been bored at Eclipse? He hadn't thought so. But now, seeing just the little he had of what went on outside the estate's walls, he knew he'd never be satisfied to seclude himself in there again. It was *too* peaceful, *too* quiet. Now he knew there were lots of interesting places to go and interesting people to meet, even if going and meeting did lead to conflict.

"I don't know much about conflict," he finally said.

"Thank your lucky stars," Sunnie said. "But don't forget, you're getting a crash course in it from Bart and Bernie. When you're through with them, you'll have a Ph.D. in conflict."

"You think so?"

"You'd better if we're going to protect your darling family from them. And it's not just your family anymore, either. It's you and Opal—did you see the way Bart looked at her when she threw him out of Walnut Manor?—and probably all of us now that they know we're on your side. They're bad clear through, and they won't stop until they get what they want or until we make them stop."

Sandy shivered.

"Right," Sunnie said. "We've all been out here long enough. We need some hot chocolate—with marshmallows, of course—and a fire. But first I want to get my camera and take pictures of every one of these snow people. I feel like I know them all because I know their parents."

That night, after dinner, Sunnie turned off the TV in the library, took up her copy of *The Wind in the Willows*, which she was reading for the second time because everybody loved it so much, and led the way upstairs to the sleepers' room. Sandy had lit the fire and arranged the chairs for her. It would be the first time she had read without the TV playing in the background. There were only the hiss and crack of the burning logs in the grate and the cottony silence that came from Walnut Manor's being enveloped in falling snow.

The solemnity of sharing a room with four comatose fellow creatures affected all the inmates. They settled themselves quietly and, though the lack of a TV screen clearly made Virgil and Lyle uneasy, they all turned their faces expectantly toward Sunnie.

She read the chapter where Rat and Mole are heading back to Rat's riverbank home, where they both now live, through a mid-December snowstorm and stumble upon Mole's old home. Rat and Mole stay the night there—fixing a cozy supper for the mice who come along caroling—and Mole realizes that, though he has a new life now, "it was good to think he had this to come back to, this place which was all his own, these things which were so glad to see him again and could always be counted upon for the same simple welcome."

When Sunnie read those words and closed the book, there was a long thoughtful silence. Could any of the people in the room have said the words Mole had?

Perhaps because of their preoccupation with their own thoughts about what constituted home, no one had noticed that while Sunnie was reading, Louie had jumped into L. Barlow Van Dyke's lap, curled himself up, and gone to sleep while Mr. Van Dyke scratched his ears.

14

Sometime during the night the power went off at Eclipse, and Sandy and Bentley awoke shivering. They dressed quickly and warmly. Bentley covered his chemistry experiments with thermal blankets, and they decided to have breakfast at Walnut Manor.

When they arrived at Walnut Manor, Sandy was surprised to find icicles hanging above the front door. On the inside.

He could see his breath in the front hall.

"Rats," Sandy said, "the heat's off here, too. It's even colder than at Eclipse."

They went upstairs, where Sunnie, in her snowsuit and mittens, had piled more blankets on the sleepers and had just thrown more logs on the grate in the fireplace. "Do you know how long it'll be before the electricity's back on?" she asked Sandy and Bentley. "We haven't got any heat or lights or kitchen appliances. Not that we need refrigeration, that's for sure. But poor Virgil and Lyle are going crazy without their TV."

"I have no idea," Bentley said. "We don't have a radio or a TV, and our phone is out, too."

"The wires to both Eclipse and Walnut Manor must have come down in the storm. There's nothing else out here, so it'll probably take a long time for the power company to pay any attention to us," Sunnie said. "They don't know we have medical equipment to worry about."

"I didn't see any wires down," Bentley said. "And I looked when we drove over here. I wonder . . ."

Bentley and Sandy looked at each other, the same idea occurring to each of them at the same time. "Bart and Bernie," they said in unison.

"No!" Sunnie said. "They wouldn't."

"Why not?" Sandy asked her. "You said yesterday that none of us were safe now. Freezing Horatio and Mousey are all that's necessary, but I doubt they'd care if a few more of us froze in our sleep. Especially me."

Sunnie put her hands on her hips. "Well, if that's what they have in mind, they've got another think coming. We're all tougher than that. Sandy, you and Graham get outside and chop lots of wood for the fireplaces. We can stay warm and cook, too. Opal's got candles and the pantry's full. All the important medical equipment's got battery backups and there're plenty of blankets. How do you think people got along before there was electricity?"

"I'm going to have a look at the telephone and power lines," Bentley said, "to see if I can find out what happened."

Graham was so terribly clumsy at chopping wood that Sandy was afraid he would amputate something on himself or on somebody else, but he kept gamely at it. Sandy wasn't so coordinated himself at first, but he caught on after a while. Everett helped, too, grunting with each stroke of the ax. Since Everett didn't attribute his grunts to anyone, Sandy knew nobody else could have said it better.

Rather than leave the sleepers alone, Sunnie and Opal decided everyone should congregate in the sickroom. Lyle and Virgil and Boom-Boom, Mr. Moreland and Mr. Van Dyke and Dr. Waldemar formed a sort of bucket brigade going up the stairs and passed along the logs and food and supplies until everything they needed was stockpiled in the hall outside the sickroom door.

Virgil and Lyle, huddled under so many blankets that they looked like a year's worth of undone laundry, asked plaintively, "When will the TV be back on?"

"I don't know," Sunnie said. "Maybe not for a long time. This might be a good chance for you to begin reading some books. I have lots and I'd love to share. And the library's full, if you don't like my books."

Mr. Moreland and Mr. Van Dyke were already browsing through Sunnie's library of financial books, blowing dust off the tops of them. Sunnie's interest in finance had flagged early, and she'd moved on to reading about gemstones in spite of the fact that Mr. Moreland told her they were a risky investment.

Soon, between the fire and the heat generated by all

their bodies, the room warmed. Opal made hot choc-olate and soup, Sunnie passed out books, and Dr. Waldemar fell asleep in his chair. When Sunnie wasn't tending to her patients, she was rubbing liniment into the shoulders of Everett and Graham, who were sore from chopping wood.

Sandy watched and regretted that his regular work-outs in the gym at Eclipse had kept him in such good shape that his own shoulders felt perfectly fine.

Late in the afternoon, Bentley returned. He came into the sickroom so red faced and angry that he looked as if he could heat the room all by himself.

"What?" Sandy said.

"Those #*@!* uncles of yours!" Bentley exploded, getting so tangled up in unwinding his scarf that he almost strangled himself. As Sunnie helped him get his scarf and coat off without hurting himself, Bentley told them what he had found out. "None of the wires are down, or even out of order. I went over every inch of them, from where they leave the poles at the road to where they come into the houses. Then I drove along Old Country Road looking for a place they might be downed. No soap. I ended up driving all the way to Jupiter and not finding anything. As long as I was in town, I went to the power company and the phone com-pany to find out about getting our service restored, and they said our service had somehow been inadvertently shut off. They blamed it on a computer error. Sort of a big coincidence that both companies shut both of us off at the same time, isn't it?"

"But how could Bart and Bernie get to the computers? Maybe it *was* an error," Sandy said.

"I don't believe it," Bentley said. "I know Bart and Bernie aren't smart enough to work a computer, but they're certainly smart enough to find somebody who can: either employees at the phone company and the utilities company, or one of their unsavory friends. For enough money, almost anybody will do almost anything. I *know* they're responsible for this. I'll bet they'd be calling right now to see if anybody answered the phone, if they knew our phones were working again, the way they did the morning after they brought the birthday cake to Eclipse."

"Are they?" Opal asked. "Working again?"

Bentley picked up the extension in the sickroom. "Yes! There's a dial tone. So we should have heat soon, too, and—" He flipped the light switch and the overhead light went on.

Sunnie hugged him. "Oh, Bentley, you've saved us."

In spite of the restoration of lights and heat, no one seemed eager to leave the sickroom, not even Lyle and Virgil. They all had the somewhat giddy feeling of accident survivors, and they needed to keep telling one another the story of what had happened to them.

When night came and their picnic-style dinner was finished, Sandy and Bentley got ready to return to Eclipse. Sandy never could explain what made him do what he did: It might have been a simple desire to share what was his with people he cared about. Anyway, he said, "Would any of you like to come spend the night at Eclipse? We have lots of beds."

Boom-Boom grabbed a handful of Sunnie's sweater and sucked hard on his thumb. Virgil and Lyle shook their heads in perfect three-quarter time. Graham went to stand by the window and look out onto the white landscape. Everett seemed to be rifling his mind for an appropriate quotation, but nothing surfaced.

"Sure," Mr. Moreland said, breaking the silence. "I'd be delighted to get out of here."

At those words, Dr. Waldemar gathered himself together and said, "I'm sure there's something in our by-laws or in our rules of operation or whatever it's called about inmates leaving the premises. Especially without permission."

Opal, whose usual crusty behavior hadn't been improved by her having quit smoking, snapped, "I give 'em permission. Attempted murder by freezing doesn't happen every day. There must be a provision for extraordinary circumstances. If this doesn't qualify, I don't know what would. Go on, all of you."

Boom-Boom continued sucking, and Virgil and Lyle continued shaking their heads, and Graham continued looking out the windows; but Everett and Mr. Moreland and Mr. Van Dyke stood up and buttoned their coats.

"Wait," Dr. Waldemar protested feebly. "I don't think . . ."

"So don't start now," Opal said gruffly. "Let 'em

go. It can get pretty boring hanging out here all the time. I've noticed that, even if you haven't."

"You want to come, too?" Sandy asked Opal.

Neither Sandy nor Sunnie missed the changing expressions on Opal's face. First there was apprehension that equaled Virgil's and Lyle's. Then consideration, anticipation, rejection, and finally, world-class grouchiness. "I can't," Opal said. "I have to take care of the place."

"I can do it," Sunnie said. "At least until morning. Go ahead, Opal. You've earned it if anybody has."

"Well . . . ," she said, badly tempted and fighting her qualms and her conscience.

Mr. Moreland came up to her, buttoned the coat she hadn't taken off all day, and, grasping her by the shoulders, pointed her toward the door. "Let's go," he said. "You can't stop to consider in the middle of a jailbreak."

"Is that what we're doing?" Opal asked, sounding uncertain for the first time in anyone's memory.

"Isn't that what it feels like?" Mr. Moreland asked.

" 'Liberty is always dangerous, but it is the safest thing we have.' Harry Emerson Fosdick," Everett said.

"Harry Emerson *Fosdick*?" Mr. Moreland asked as they went out the door. "I'm starting to think you make these things up."

After they left, Sunnie sent everyone else off to get ready for bed. When they were gone and she had the first quiet moment she'd had all day, she tried to remember if she had actually seen Louie sitting in L. Barlow Van Dyke the cat molester's lap last night or if she had just imagined it.

Sunnie was serving a cereal-and-muffin breakfast in the sickroom the next morning when she heard a loud commotion downstairs.

"Graham," she said, "go see what's going on." When Graham looked at her, uncertain and a little frightened, she added, "Boom-Boom, you go with him. I'm sure the two of you together will be perfectly capable of finding out what's happening."

Boom-Boom took his thumb out of his mouth and said proudly, in his grown-up voice, "Come along, Graham. We must look out for Sunnie and our sleepers." He hesitated briefly in the doorway, and his thumb headed for his mouth. But then he squared his shoulders and went off down the hall, with Graham two steps behind him.

Sunnie stood in the doorway of the sickroom listening. She heard shouting from downstairs, and she recognized Sandy's voice and Mr. Moreland's and Opal's. She didn't recognize the other voices. The noise went on for quite a while until suddenly the front door slammed with a crash that shook the entire building. Then there was total silence for a moment before she heard the pounding of a lot of feet running up the stairs.

She closed the sickroom door, locked it, and stood with her back braced against it. If that was Bart and

Bernie on the way upstairs, they'd have to get past her before they could get to her sleepers, or to Eddy, or Virgil and Lyle, or Dr. Waldemar.

Pounding on the door shook her so hard her teeth rattled, but she continued to lean against the door panels as Virgil, Lyle, and Dr. Waldemar cowered together.

"Sunnie, it's me, Sandy. Open up."

With relief, Sunnie unlocked the door and was almost knocked down as Sandy, Bentley, Mr. Moreland, Mr. Van Dyke, Opal, Everett, Graham, and Boom-Boom rushed into the room, all talking at once.

"Stop!" she screamed over the clamor. "I can't hear anything you're saying."

"Quite right," Bentley said, smoothing his overcoat lapels. "Sandy, you tell."

Everyone crowded around Sunnie and Sandy, who stood facing each other in the crush.

"As I drove up Old Country Road from Eclipse, I saw a car coming from the other direction. It turned into Walnut Manor just ahead of me. I guess I shouldn't have been surprised when Bart and Bernie got out of it, but I was. But that was nothing compared to how surprised they were when I got out of the Daimler, and then Bentley, Opal, Mr. Moreland, Mr. Van Dyke, and Everett did, too. They looked as if they were seeing ghosts, which is probably what they were *hoping* to see inside. Opal lit right into them and ordered them off the property."

"She's just crabby because she hasn't had a cigarette

in a few weeks," Mr. Moreland said. "Crabbier than usual, I mean."

Opal stuck her elbow into Mr. Moreland's stomach and said, "Three weeks, six days, eleven hours, and fourteen minutes."

Sandy continued. "They said they were going to report Bentley and me for kidnapping inmates or encouraging a breakout or something equally felonious, and that we'd be locked up so fast it would make our heads swim and we'd never have a chance to spend all Horatio's money. As if that's what we wanted to do."

"We'll just say nothing ever happened," Mr. Moreland said. "There's no evidence to substantiate their accusations."

"But isn't that lying?" Sandy asked. He'd never told a lie, though he knew what they were.

"Certainly not," Mr. Moreland answered indignantly. "Nobody was kidnapped and there was no breakout. In court, all you have to do is answer the questions they ask you, yes or no. Don't elaborate or you'll get yourself in trouble."

"Your uncles are getting desperate," Sunnie said, sounding worried.

"They're desperate and *dumb*," Opal said. "A dangerous combination. I think we'd better be prepared for something really drastic next time."

They all knew there would be a next time.

CHAPTER

15

- - - - - - -

In order to distract them all from worrying, Sunnie got the inmates to assemble Christmas presents for one another, and Opal began complicated preparations for a Christmas Eve feast. Everyone had an opinion as to what should be served. Boom-Boom wanted roast beef with Yorkshire pudding and chocolate-chip cookies. Mr. Moreland wanted champagne and caviar. Dr. Waldemar wanted sauerbraten and marzipan. Virgil and Lyle wanted meat loaf and mashed potatoes. Everett wanted madeleines because Proust liked them. Mr. Van Dyke and Eddy wouldn't say what they wanted, and Graham wanted it all.

So Opal decided to make it all, but only if everyone would help her. Bentley ordered the supplies from the fanciest grocery in Jupiter, and for many days in advance, when the inmates weren't keeping secrets from each other about their presents, they were in the kitchen helping Opal chop and stir and cook and freeze things. Graham was one of Opal's most ardent helpers, and he always came out of the kitchen a little fatter than when he went in.

Finally Sunnie felt she had to take him in hand. "Graham," she said, "each time you go into the kitchen, I want you to lift everything in the dining room on the way in and on the way out. You can make that your Christmas present to me."

"That's a strange present," he said. "Why would you want that?"

"Never mind. I just do. Will you give it to me?"

"I guess so. Does that mean every fork and spoon, one at a time?"

"Only if you can't figure out a more efficient way to do it."

"Oh," he said, and she could almost hear the wheels turn inside his head. "So if I can lift the whole table, I've also lifted everything that's on it?"

"Why, what a smart idea," Sunnie told him. "That would make it much faster, wouldn't it?"

Graham rose to the challenge. The first time he tried it, crouching underneath the table and straining upward with it resting on his back, he could barely get the table legs off the ground. He was so fat that just getting underneath the table in the first place represented a considerable amount of exercise. He couldn't lift the sideboard all at once, so he had to take the drawers out, lift them individually, and then try to get the sideboard up. Lifting the chairs was a snap.

Soon, he could pile two or three chairs together and lift them at once. Then he could put a couple of chairs on top of the table and lift them together. Then he could put all the chairs on the table. Then he could lift the sideboard with the drawers out. Then, with the drawers in.

He barely noticed that it was becoming easier for him to get beneath the table. But he did notice, finally, that his belt wasn't on the last hole anymore. And that his shirts, while still tight around the shoulders, were flapping at the waist.

"Look, Sunnie!" he said, running across her in the dining room on the morning of Christmas Eve. "Look at my belt! What happened?"

"You've been getting a lot of exercise," she said. "And staying out of the kitchen while you did it. Less food and more exercise makes you lose weight. It isn't magic. You did it all by yourself. Aren't you proud? And there's no reason why you can't keep on doing what you've been doing—you can lift the library stuff and the bedroom stuff, as well as the dining room stuff, you know. You'll be able to wear a bathing suit when the pool gets filled in the summer. You can leave here."

Graham had looked ecstatic until Sunnie mentioned leaving Walnut Manor. Then the expression on his face approached panic. "If I get thin, do I *have* to leave?" His eyes darted in the direction of the kitchen.

"Don't you want to go home?"

"Would *you* want to go back to two people who were so embarrassed by the way you looked that they hid you? And then never came to see you or even sent a card?"

"You've got a point," Sunnie had to admit. "Well, the way I see it, you can stay here as long as you like. Nobody can *make* you leave."

"Are you sure?"

"I'm positive," she said, even though she wasn't. She couldn't see the harm in giving Graham hope and encouragement. Those were things everybody needed, and Graham had had far less of them than he was entitled to.

"When you said I should lift everything in the dining room, did you mean *everything*?" he asked her.

"Sure," she said.

So he picked her up and carried her into the library, where he set her down in a chair and then lifted her *and* the chair.

That night they gathered in a dining room transformed by candlelight and Christmas decorations.

Boom-Boom was so entranced, he couldn't eat. Mr. Moreland grumbled about not being able to see his food, but it didn't matter because he wouldn't be able to remember what he'd eaten anyway. Everett kept saying, "God bless us, every one," while Dr. Waldemar speculated whether using candles every night would significantly reduce the electricity bill.

Bentley and Sandy remembered happy Christmases at Eclipse, and neither could tell if the shine in the other's eyes came from tears or from candle glow.

Sandy thought Sunnie looked like an angel, with the candlelight reflecting off her white uniform and silvery hair. If Mousey and Horatio and Flossie and Attila were with them around the table, it would have been the most perfect Christmas of Sandy's life.

They toasted each other with wine that Bentley had brought from Eclipse's cellars, scornfully leaving behind, in the darkest corner, the inferior bottle of port Bart and Bernie had brought last fall.

Everett raised his glass and said, " 'True friendship is like sound health, the value of it is seldom known until it be lost.' Charles Caleb Colton. 1780 to 1832."

"I know how much I value all of you," Sunnie said. "And I don't have to lose you to know that. I hope I never have to know what it feels like to be without your friendship."

None of the inmates had ever had such words addressed to them, and Sunnie's declaration took them by such surprise that they were speechless. Ditto for Dr. Waldemar and Opal. There were sounds of swallowing and throat clearing and even a sniff or two before Opal said, in the softest, friendliest voice anyone had ever heard her use, "Have some seconds before the feast gets cold."

After dinner they all went up to the sickroom to watch as Bentley administered another of his experiments to Attila. His last experiment had turned her feathers blue, but the color had finally worn off. He felt that she was ready for another try.

They all held their breaths as he squeezed an eye-dropperful of something sticky and purple into her beak. Attila hiccuped. It was the first sound any of the sleepers had made in months. Could it mean she was waking up? Wouldn't that be the best Christmas present ever?

After they had stood around her dishpan listening to her hiccup for an hour, they had to conclude that her *hics* did not mean she was waking up. All they meant was that she had the hiccups. Bentley was so disappointed, he almost wept. Not only hadn't he found a cure for the comas, but what he had developed wouldn't be useful in any way. Who would buy a concoction that induced hiccups in chickens?

Glumly, Sandy and Bentley returned to Eclipse, and Opal and Sunnie saw everyone else off to bed.

The next morning in the library—with a blazing fire, a Christmas tree, and a view through the French doors of the snow-covered stone porch and garden beyond— it was possible to believe that Santa Claus actually had paid Walnut Manor a visit. For the first time ever, there were presents under the tree besides the boxes of candy that Dr. Waldemar always gave everyone. Sunnie gave books, Everett gave beautifully hand-lettered quotations, and Virgil and Lyle gave Couch Potato membership patches. Graham had spent hours in the unheated barn, with the cow and chickens for company, making keepsake boxes with parquetry lids. Mr. Van Dyke had ordered mugs with each person's name. No one knew where Opal had found the time to knit them each a pair of mittens, and everyone was surprised at the cashmere mufflers Mr. Moreland had had delivered from the city for them all. With his white beard, he almost looked like Santa as he passed out the packages. "So we can build a whole metropolis of snow people without getting sore throats," he said gruffly.

Boom-Boom's gifts were bottles of bubble-blowing liquid he had added to the weekly phone-in grocery order one day when Opal wasn't paying attention. Poor Eddy could only watch, but watch he did, especially the clouds of shimmering bubbles that, thanks to Boom-Boom, Virgil, and Lyle, floated around the library all day.

Sandy and Bentley had spent hours discussing what their gifts should be. Neither of them were used to giving gifts, since they hadn't celebrated birthdays at Eclipse and had honored Christmas only with feasting and music. But the planning made Bentley remember the pleasure associated with trying to express affection with a present, and he taught it to Sandy.

Bentley decided to give rides to the inmates in the Daimler, as far up Old Country Road as the passenger wanted to go.

"But aren't we already in enough trouble for taking Mr. Moreland and Mr. Van Dyke and Everett and Opal to Eclipse?" Sandy asked. "Bart and Bernie may still report us for that."

Bentley shrugged. "Might as well be hanged for a goat as a sheep, or whatever that saying is. I should ask Everett. How much more trouble can I get in for doing the same thing again? These folks have been locked up in here too long. I want to spring them, just for a little while."

Sandy couldn't decide what his presents should be since he'd never given any before, except that they should be something extra special. Everything he thought of seemed inadequate.

Finally he had decided to write letters, telling each person what he or she had done or said that had had special meaning to him. He even wrote one to Eddy, whom Sandy had come to see as patient and steady and a good audience, and without whom their little group would seem incomplete. He addressed the letters and put Christmas seals in the corners to make them look like real letters with stamps that had actually gone through the mail.

Throughout Christmas day, and for days afterward, Sandy saw different inmates take his letters from their pockets and read them over and over again. He was glad he'd used his heavy imported stationery and his fancy fountain pen.

He wrote Sunnie a letter, too, telling her how much he appreciated the tender care she had taken of his family and how much he had learned from knowing her. He had another gift he wanted to give her, as well, but for that he had to wait until the end of Christmas Day.

Bentley spent most of the afternoon chauffeuring. Eventually everyone took a ride. Opal and Mr. Moreland went together, and they were gone the longest. Bentley said he'd taken them halfway to Jupiter. Lyle and Virgil, after much urging and cajoling, went as far as Eclipse, but only with Sunnie sitting between them, holding their hands.

Even Eddy was loaded into the backseat, with Graham to hold him steady and Everett to offer him quotes about adventure and courage.

Boom-Boom had needed almost as much persuading as Virgil and Lyle, but once he was in the car, he wanted to push every button, turn every dial, and then go along on everyone else's ride, too.

Christmas Day was the most exciting holiday any of them had had for a long time, what with the bubbles, the rides, the real letters, and all the other gifts. The excitement helped them to forget that the sleepers still slept, and Attila still hiccuped.

At last the dinner dishes had been washed and dried and put away, and Sandy gathered his presents and asked Sunnie to walk him to the door. Bentley had already put on his new mittens and wrapped his new scarf around his neck and gone to start the Daimler.

"Wasn't this a wonderful day?" Sunnie asked Sandy as they stood in the front hall. "I know that sounds funny when we're in a place like this and your family is in the condition they're in, but we still had fun. I don't know how to explain it."

"I think anything's bearable if you have the right people to bear it with you," Sandy said.

"Why, of course, that's it," Sunnie said. "The right people make all the difference. Thank you again for your sweet letter. It's been my privilege to be your family's nurse, and I don't need any thanks. But it's good to get them anyway."

"I have another present for you besides the letter," Sandy said, taking a small box out of his pocket.

"Oh, that's not at all necessary," she told him. "I've already had the best Christmas of my life."

"I know it's not necessary," Sandy told her. "I wanted to do it." He put the little box in her hand.

"Well, thank you," she said solemnly as she opened it. "Oh, Sandy, it's beautiful." On a pad of cotton lay a small gold signet ring with an *S* in fancy script on the face of it and a tiny diamond at each end of the *S*.

"It was my baby ring," Sandy said. "And our initials are the same."

"Well, it's just gorgeous," she said, slipping it onto her finger and holding out her hand so that the hall light struck the ring and made it shine. "Did you know that diamonds, since they crystallize in the isometric crystal system, are optically isotropic, though anomalous double refractions caused by strain are often noted?"

Sandy noticed that Sunnie's voice trembled. "No," he said, "I didn't know that. But you've been reading about gemstones, so I'm not surprised you know it."

"I just don't know what it means," she said, looking up at him. The two generous tears that spilled down her cheeks were bigger and shinier than the diamonds in the ring and caused a change in the pattern of Sandy's heartbeats that the diamonds never had.

"Don't cry," he said, taking her shoulders gently in his hands.

"I can't help it," she said, as two more tears followed. "My heart is so full, I guess the fullness has to leak out."

Sandy's heart was full, too, of strange and bewildering sensations. Somehow, instinctively, he knew what to do about them. He bent his head and kissed Sunnie's soft mouth. And right away learned a whole lot of new and astonishing feelings.

He raised his head just as Bentley tooted the horn of the Daimler. "I have to go," he said. "I'll see you tomorrow."

Sunnie raised her hand to her lips, and all the way back to Eclipse, that's the way Sandy saw her in his mind: her eyes big and round and blue and her fingers touching his kiss, while a *cirrostratus nebulosus* of bubbles swirled around her.

CHAPTER

16

- - - - - - -

During the short cold days and long cold nights of January, Sandy sat at the card table playing Investment—as they had renamed their altered Monopoly game—with Mr. Moreland and Mr. Van Dyke. Sunnie's vitamins must have been having an effect, because Mr. Moreland remembered more and more of his financial knowledge and he transmitted it to Sandy in lucid installments.

Bentley worked feverishly on his coma cures but succeeded only in developing something that eliminated Attila's hiccups and another that eliminated all her feathers. Opal gave him several pieces of her mind about doing that to poor Attila during the coldest month of the year, and then stayed up all night to knit a sweater to keep Attila warm.

Sunnie never sat on the arm of Sandy's chair anymore when he played Investment, and she was subdued, though pleasant, when he visited her and his family in the sickroom in the mornings. Although he knew he would never forget what it had felt like to kiss her, he was sorry he had, since that had apparently caused a coolness between them. He was too inexperienced to know how to fix it. All he could do was watch her with his sad eyes, which she wouldn't meet. She didn't wear the signet ring, either.

He knew she was busy: She had her sleepers. She had snow-person-building sessions every afternoon. She was always taking walks with Virgil and Lyle, who were watching less TV lately, or playing games with Boom-Boom, who had graduated from Candyland and Go Fish to gin rummy and Clue and, recently, to poker and the old Monopoly; or she was being carried around unexpectedly by Graham, who could now lift every piece of furniture in Walnut Manor, and sometimes several pieces at once, and whose clothes were held on by safety pins; or she was talking to Eddy, or reading stories to them all. No wonder she had no time for Sandy.

But before the kiss, somehow there had been time.

The one thing they all did was wait: wait for the next salvo from Bart and Bernie; wait for the board of directors to show up and do something about the kidnapping charge Bart and Bernie had threatened to bring against them.

Nothing happened. And the waiting was making them all jumpy as crickets.

Opal had caught up on her indoor chores and couldn't do any gardening until spring, so she took to hanging around the Investment game to keep her mind occupied. She hadn't had a cigarette in weeks, and had almost stopped keeping an unlit one in her mouth. She chewed gum instead.

"Frisk it all!" Mr. Moreland said one day as he sat trying to play Investment, with Opal cracking her gum in his ear. "Are you trying to deafen me, woman?"

"Obviously I'm not succeeding," she answered.

"I can't concentrate worth a dalmatian with you doing that." He threw his cards onto the table and stood up. "And I'm bored with this game, anyway. I wish I had some real money to play with now that I remember what to do with it."

Mr. Van Dyke pantomimed opening a book.

"What?" Mr. Moreland said. "You'd rather read a book?"

Mr. Van Dyke started turning red as he shook his head and made more incomprehensible gestures.

"You want to churn butter? You want to blow up vegetables? What? I can't understand your signals." Mr. Moreland was getting red in the face, too.

"I think he's trying to say something about looking at a business's books," Sandy said. Mr. Van Dyke nodded his head vigorously. "You mean Walnut Manor's books?" Sandy asked him. Again Mr. Van Dyke nodded.

"Hot damask!" Mr. Moreland said. "Why didn't I think of that? He's right, Sandy. Your financial education isn't complete until you've had a look at a real set of books, balance sheets, statements, all that stuff. And Doc's got an office full of them right across the hall."

"Good luck," Opal said. "He hasn't looked at any

of it himself in years. He knew without looking that we were getting barely enough money to scrape along, so why should he waste his time plowing through the gobbledygook the board of directors sends us to find out what he already knew? Especially when he could be taking a perfectly good nap. There's a whole file cabinet of unopened records in there. That should keep your mind off the sound of my gum for a good long time."

Mr. Moreland was so excited he whipped right over to the chair in which Dr. Waldemar was sleeping and shook him awake. "Okay if we have a look at Walnut Manor's financial statements, Doc? For educational purposes?"

Dr. Waldemar, barely awake, nodded drowsily, and then his chin dropped back onto his chest.

"You come along, Graham," Mr. Moreland said, taking charge the way he used to before he'd had to move to Walnut Manor. "I want you to bring a file cabinet in here from Doc's office. His office is too small for all of us to work in."

Graham hitched up his safety-pinned pants and swaggered importantly into the office. After a couple of attempts, he managed to get the file cabinet across his back and, with muscles bulging he hadn't had even a few weeks ago, he conveyed it to the library.

Like boys in a candy store, Mr. Moreland and Mr. Van Dyke dived into the drawers of the cabinet, pulling out unopened packages and envelopes, and scattering them on top of the Investment game on the card table, as well as all over the floor.

"Let's get them in chronological order first," Mr. Moreland said. "*Then*, Sandy, my boy, your financial education will go into high gear."

By the next afternoon, Sandy was more confused than ever. Mr. Moreland and Mr. Van Dyke didn't seem to be in much better shape.

"I swear, L. Barlow," Mr. Moreland said, "I thought my memory was getting better, but I can't make heads or tails out of all this. None of these numbers makes any sense at all."

L. Barlow Van Dyke had a blizzard of papers spread out in front of him on top of the buried Investment game. He squinted and turned the papers around and squinted some more. Suddenly his eyebrows went up and he handed a couple of sheets of paper across the table to Mr. Moreland. He pointed to several places, poking so hard he almost made holes in the papers.

"What?" Mr. Moreland asked. "You don't understand this? Neither do I."

Mr. Van Dyke turned red and shook his head and poked the papers violently again.

"You're killing a bug? You're doing exercises? What?"

"I think he wants you to notice something," Sandy said.

"Well, shingles! I sure am getting tired of these games of charades we keep playing." He peered closely at the papers for quite some time, while Mr. Van Dyke tapped his fingers impatiently on the pile in front of him and scowled.

All at once Mr. Moreland's eyebrows went up, too. He and Mr. Van Dyke looked at each other across the table with delight, and they both laughed.

"These books have been cooked," Mr. Moreland exclaimed.

"They're cookbooks?" Sandy asked, more confused than ever. "I thought they were business books."

"They are," Mr. Moreland said. "But somebody's been cooking them, altering them, playing with the numbers. Somebody's been embezzling Walnut Manor's money for a long time! No wonder this place is scraping along. Somebody's gotten very rich on our fees."

By the time he finished saying this, everybody in the library, except Dr. Waldemar, was clustered around the card table.

"Who?" Sandy asked. "Surely not Dr. Waldemar."

They all turned to look at Dr. Waldemar, who snored peacefully away in his chair before the fire.

"Absolutely not," Mr. Moreland said. He began scrabbling through the pile of papers. "Where's that list of the board of directors?"

L. Barlow scrabbled along with him until they found what they were looking for. Quickly they both scanned the list of names, then looked at each other with perfect understanding. Mr. Moreland handed the list to Graham. "Read that list and tell me if you recognize any names on it. Then pass it along."

Graham read the list and said, in a shocked voice, "My father's name is there."

As the others read the list, they discovered that one of Virgil's and Lyle's sisters was on the list, Everett's wife, Boom-Boom's mother. Eddy couldn't tell them anything, but they assumed that the one remaining name was related to him somehow.

"Who do you know on the list?" Sandy asked Mr. Moreland.

"My brother-in-law."

"How about Mr. Van Dyke?" Graham asked.

Mr. Moreland shook his head almost unbelievingly. "His son."

"You mean," Sandy began, "you mean, your relatives have been paying your fees here and then getting most of the money back?"

Mr. Moreland nodded. Sandy had expected an explosion of Mr. Moreland's synthetic swear words or a tantrum or *something* dramatic. What he wasn't prepared for was the terrible sadness he read on Mr. Moreland's face. Mr. Van Dyke was bright red, but he looked sad, too.

As Sandy looked at the circle of faces around the table, he saw the same woeful expression appear on all of them as the realization penetrated that their families had given them away and that the surrender had not been difficult, either emotionally or financially.

Mr. Moreland took up a pencil and began figuring. "They paid Walnut Manor's whopping fees, left fifteen percent of them for Opal and Dr. Waldemar to scrape along on, stole back the other eighty-five percent, which, invested at a modest eight percent—and undoubtedly more, the way the market's gone lately—would yield, over ten years . . ." He scribbled for a minute and then held up the paper. "Look at that! They've gotten rid of us *and* gotten rich. And probably claimed some kind of tax write-off, too, for something or other. My brother-in-law works for the IRS—Lord knows how he's been able to use that—but I'm betting none of this income has been reported. I can't even guess how many laws have been violated here."

"I don't care," Boom-Boom said, sticking his thumb in his mouth, as he had not done (except at bedtime) for several weeks. "I like it better here, anyway."

"That may be true," Boom-Boom said, in his grown-up voice, after removing his thumb. "But a crime has been committed and we must see that it is punished."

"That's right," Graham said. "We can't let them get away with this. Besides, it's insulting that they would think Dr. Waldemar was so stupid that he wouldn't notice what was going on." They all looked at the snoring Dr. Waldemar. "Maybe not stupid," Graham amended, "but . . . distracted."

"Like we all are. Were," Virgil said.

"Were is right," Lyle added. "But not anymore. I don't feel nearly as distracted as I used to."

"But you've got a point," Mr. Moreland said, pulling thoughtfully on his beard. "Who's going to listen to anything we have to say? We're only a bunch of nuts.

How can we report a crime? The board, our loving relatives, will just say we're out of our minds. And I'm not sure Dr. Waldemar would have much more credibility than we would. Especially when it comes out that he hasn't looked at any of the board's reports for years."

"And if you do report this crime and aren't believed," Opal said, "you won't have only Bart and Bernie after you. You'll have the whole board. Once they know you're on to them, do you think they'll be satisfied with keeping you stashed away here in the country? They'd probably rather have you playing harps."

"Or stoking fires," Mr. Moreland muttered.

" 'Those who welcome death have only tried it from the ears up.' Wilson Mizner," Everett said.

As they pondered this, the front doorbell rang, making them all jump eight inches in the air. Opal, who was extra nervous to begin with because of quitting smoking, jumped eleven.

Opal tiptoed to the front door and peeked out the side window. "It's only the grocery delivery boy," she called back to those crowded in the library doorway. "We're still safe."

Graham came to the door, dismissed the delivery boy, and managed to carry all the boxes of groceries, in a pile, to the kitchen in one trip.

None of them liked knowing that a simple grocery delivery could scare them half out of their wits—especially now that they were getting their wits back.

When Sunnie came downstairs for lunch, it was a morose group she found by the library fire. Mr.

Moreland and Mr. Van Dyke, and even Sandy, stirred disconsolately through the pile of financial papers. Now that they knew what they were looking for, they found ever more evidence to support what they knew to be true. They even turned up a threatening letter from the board about Bentley and Sandy taking the inmates to Eclipse the night the power had been off. Dr. Waldemar hadn't opened it, so they'd missed knowing that, if it happened again, legal action would be brought. Good thing the board didn't know about the Christmas rides.

Virgil and Lyle sat staring at a blank TV screen. They were so upset, they hadn't remembered to turn it on. Boom-Boom paced, his hands clasped desperately behind his back so he wouldn't suck his thumb. Everett muttered and mumbled quotations that only he could hear. And Graham stood looking out the French doors onto the snow, absentmindedly lifting Opal in an armchair. Dr. Waldemar slept on.

"Gee, everybody's so quiet," Sunnie said, not meeting Sandy's eyes, even though he gazed intently at her. "Have we got the winter blues? You know, there are people who get that way when they don't see the sun enough. They get depressed and sad and sleep all the time. And do you know what the cure is? Light. That's all. Just light. Don't you wish there were a simple cure for everything? Oh, I wish there were a simple cure for comas. I seem to have a touch of the blues myself today. What can we do to cheer ourselves up? How about turning all the lights on?"

"The lights are already on," Opal said. Graham had

stopped lifting her chair and had slid down to sit on the floor. "I don't think light is going to fix the problem we've got today."

"You shouldn't be negative," Sunnie said, sitting on the couch next to Virgil, whose head had fallen onto Lyle's shoulder. Lyle's own head rested on the couch back and they both snored lightly—nothing to compete with Dr. Waldemar's Olympic championship snoring. "It's important to give things a chance. Then once you've tried them, you can decide if they work or not." Opal yawned, which Sunnie thought was rather rude, though she knew Opal's manners weren't always the best. Besides, she tried to make allowances for Opal now that she'd quit smoking. Rudeness wasn't fatal as often as cigarette smoking was.

Yawning was one thing, but when Opal's eyes closed, Sunnie felt justified in being hurt. She thought what she was saying was pretty interesting. Maybe she should try talking about something else. "Where's Bentley?" she asked. "Isn't he coming to lunch today?"

There was no response. From anyone. Looking around, Sunnie realized that they were all asleep: Opal in her chair; Graham on the floor; Eddy on his platform; Boom-Boom, Everett, Mr. Moreland, Mr. Van Dyke, and Sandy all slumped over onto the card table. How odd. And how odd that Sunnie herself felt so drowsy. Perhaps she wasn't getting enough sleep. Perhaps she needed more vitamins or more exercise or more . . .

CHAPTER

17

- - - - - - -

Bentley had had high hopes for his new cure. He'd even skipped lunch to keep working on it, and that was a great sacrifice because he very much enjoyed lunch at Walnut Manor. But by midafternoon it was clear to him that he was on another wild cure chase.

He poured the concoction down the sink in the little laboratory and went to the kitchen, where he fixed himself a sandwich of smoked turkey paté and poured a Pensa-Cola into a thin crystal goblet. He'd thought having a fancy lunch would cheer him up, but realized the most cheering thing he could think of was to see Flossie's face, even if she was asleep. Then to cheer himself up from seeing Flossie still asleep, he could go downstairs and talk to the others.

He left his sandwich unfinished and poured his Pensa-Cola down the sink, as he had the failed cure. Maybe Opal had made spaghetti for lunch, and maybe there would be leftovers now that Graham wasn't eating everything that wasn't glued down or hidden. He hated to admit it, but Opal's spaghetti sauce was better than his own.

Sighing, he put on his coat and went to the garage.

When Bentley came through the door at Walnut Manor, he heard a peculiar, repetitive sound that he couldn't identify. He stood in the hall, his head cocked, listening.

It wasn't the TV, he was pretty sure of that. He knew which programs Virgil and Lyle usually watched at this time, though recently in the afternoons they'd been going outdoors with Sunnie or reading to each other or helping Opal cook and clean.

He knew what it sounded like, but it couldn't possibly be a bunch of people all snoring in unison.

Could it? That's *exactly* what it sounded like.

He opened the doors to the library. The sound was louder and it *was* a bunch of people all snoring in unison.

"Hey!" he yelled. "What did Opal make for lunch? Damitol soup?"

Nobody stirred.

Bentley went to the card table and shook Sandy. Sandy slept on.

Oh, no, Bentley thought. This was like the first morning when he hadn't been able to wake Flossie. And then Horatio and Mousey. And then Attila.

He shook Mr. Moreland and Mr. Van Dyke and Everett and Boom-Boom. Nothing.

He shook Sunnie and Virgil and Lyle, Eddy and Opal and Graham. More nothing.

It was no comfort at all to Bentley that he was positive he knew who was responsible for all this snoring. He didn't know how they'd done it, but Bart and Bernie had thought of some other way to induce comas. Or worse.

He was scared and sad for a moment, and then he was so angry it frightened him. How dare Bart and Bernie be so greedy and mean and unscrupulous? How dare they think they could get away with this? He would *not* permit it.

He was so angry he was burning up with it. He tore off his coat, and he was still burning up. He flung open the French doors to the stone porch and stepped out into the snow. It took him a lot of deep, cold breaths, but finally he calmed down and went back into the library.

Imagine his surprise when he saw that Sunnie had opened her eyes and was sitting up, rubbing her temples and looking around her.

"Bentley," she said. "What's happening here?"

"I thought you would know," he said, relieved beyond words. "I just arrived and found all of you sound asleep and snoring."

"It was the oddest thing," Sunnie told him. "I sat down to talk to Opal before lunch, and she fell asleep while I was speaking. I looked around and saw that everybody else was asleep, too. And then I felt sooooo drowsy that I couldn't resist closing my eyes just for a second. What time is it?"

"Three-thirty."

Opal's eyes opened suddenly. "It's freezing in here," she complained, sitting up in her chair. "What nincompoop opened the French doors?"

Sunnie jumped off the couch and ran to her. "Bentley did, and don't call him a nincompoop. He probably saved our lives. Look—" She gestured around the room, where the sleepers were groggily beginning to wake. "Something put us all to sleep just before lunch. If it was one of Bart and Bernie's schemes, I'm sure none of us was meant to wake up." She shivered, and not just from the cold. "When Bentley opened the French doors, whatever was in the air must have drifted out, and we woke up while we still could."

Bentley searched the room but found nothing suspicious. Suddenly he exclaimed, "Flossie!" and ran out through the library doors and up the stairs to the sickroom with Sunnie right behind him.

When he flung open the sickroom door, Louie, who was sleeping at the foot of Flossie's bed, lifted his head and looked annoyed at having his nap interrupted. Bentley raced to the window and threw it open before he ran to Flossie's bed. As soon as he saw that the covers were moving up and down with her breaths, he threw his arms around her and burst into tears. Really, all those quiet years at Eclipse hadn't accustomed him to so much violent emotion, and he was finding it both dismaying and exciting.

Sunnie checked on her other patients, who were fine although still comatose. She stood and patted Bentley's back while he collected himself. "Whatever it was that put the rest of us to sleep must not have gotten up here yet. I'm going to open every window in the house and keep them open until we know what's going on. I'm scared."

"Me, too," Bentley said. "What if I hadn't come along until dinnertime? What if I'd decided to work through dinner?"

"Don't think about it," Sunnie said. "That's not what happened, and we're all OK. But we do need to find out what *did* happen. I'll stay up here; I'm not going to leave my sleepers for a moment until this is over. But you and the others must search the whole house to see if you can find anything unusual."

Bentley took a huge white handkerchief from his pocket, wiped his eyes, and was about to put it away, when Sunnie said in a quivering voice, "Can I have a corner?"

He handed her his handkerchief and watched while she dried her own eyes. Sharing one's handkerchief and one's tears makes a bond between two people that is never forgotten.

Bentley stood up, straightened his jacket, and marched downstairs.

Hours later, everyone but Sunnie and the sleepers met in the library to report what their searches had turned up. Unfortunately, everyone had found the same thing: nothing.

"Think," Sandy exhorted them. "Think *hard*. Was there *anything* the least bit unusual, anywhere?"

"Well," Graham said hesitantly, "there *was* something. It seemed so trivial I dismissed it, but since it's the only clue we've got, maybe—"

"*What!*" they all yelled.

Graham looked startled. "It was in the kitchen. You know, I am pretty familiar with the kitchen, and if I was going to notice any little thing out of the ordinary, that's where I'd notice it. What I found," he went on, "was an empty Pensa-Cola syrup canister." He stopped, as if he'd made a great announcement.

"So what?" Opal said, cracking her gum. That was the only time that those who heard it would be glad she was still alive to make that annoying sound. "We use a lot of Pensa-Cola."

"But it was in the delivery of groceries we got this morning. It should have been full. And I know it wasn't the old canister because I hauled that one out to the trash yesterday." Again he paused. And again no one could figure out why he thought this was significant.

"You mean we fell asleep because the market delivered us an empty canister of Pensa-Cola?" Mr. Moreland asked. "Bunch of poppycock, Graham. Makes no sense at all."

"No, you don't get it. I think the canister was full of some kind of gas that was released once we brought it into the house. Bentley, you know about chemistry. Is there a gas that's odorless and colorless and wouldn't leave any trace in the air or in the blood, but that could kill us if we breathed it long enough?"

Bentley thought so hard his forehead puckers took hours to smooth out. "Yes," he said finally. "It's called cyanosulfidioxinethonoxide. It completely dissipates from the air within six hours. But it's banned in this country."

"That wouldn't mean anything to Bart and Bernie," Sandy said. "They could get it somehow."

"Sounds like something in the list of ingredients on a frozen diet dinner," Graham said.

"Come to think of it," Opal said, "that grocery boy wasn't the one who usually delivers, was he? I think I'll call the market and see who made our delivery." She left the library and went to make her phone call.

"Well, if that's what happened," Sandy said, "if Bart and Bernie tried to kill us with poison gas disguised as Pensa-Cola, then they've got even more nerve than I thought. Horatio would be outraged."

"Do you think Bart and Bernie will be coming by soon to see how well their plan worked?" Virgil asked. He scooted a little closer to Lyle on the couch.

"I think they'll wait until at least tomorrow," Bentley said. "Just to make sure we're all . . . you know. There'd be no hurry."

Opal came back from the office. "I talked to the guy who usually delivers our groceries. He was just leaving to come out here when he discovered that all four tires on his van were flat. A nicely dressed man came by, told him he was headed this way, and offered to deliver the groceries for him."

"You think it was Bart or Bernie?" Graham asked.

"Maybe. Or somebody they hired," Opal said. "If it was Bart or Bernie, they had to have turned the groceries over to someone else before they got to Walnut Manor. But I'll bet anything they're the ones who substituted the poison-filled canister for the real one."

"We have no proof that's what happened, or even that that's what made you fall asleep," Bentley said, trying to be reasonable, even though they were all convinced that their theory was correct. "We'd never be able to bring these charges to court."

"It's too bad Bart and Bernie couldn't use their ingenuity to make a living the honest way," Sandy said. "They may be dumb in a lot of ways, but they've got amazing criminal creativity."

"A good reason for us all to hurry up and think of a way to stop them," Mr. Moreland said. "We might not be as lucky next time."

"I've *got* to find a cure for these comas," Bentley said. "Our poor sleepers can't protect themselves; it's up to us to watch out for them. We're responsible for what happens to them—" He shook his head and put his coat on. "I'm going back to Eclipse and get to work. You want to come, Sandy?"

"No," Sandy said. "I'll stay here. But I'll walk you to the car."

In the driveway Bentley said, "I'll see you later.

You'd better go up and tell Sunnie what we think happened."

"Oh, I'll let Graham or somebody else tell her. She doesn't seem to want to talk to me lately."

"How come?"

"I don't know," Sandy said, though he was pretty sure he did. Somehow he was embarrassed to have Bentley know about the kiss. "She probably thinks I'm boring and dull."

"I doubt it," said Bentley, who remembered enough of his own youth to know that whatever was going on between Sunnie and Sandy was more complicated than either of them knew.

One by one, all the inmates drifted upstairs to the sickroom. They didn't feel right leaving Sunnie alone, and they didn't want to be apart from one another, either.

Sunnie waited seven hours, just to be on the safe side, and then went around closing windows, cautioning everyone to speak up if they began to feel any drowsiness. They were still wide awake after dinner, so they quit worrying—at least about the gas.

Sunnie read a chapter from *Treasure Island* before Bentley came to take Sandy back to Eclipse, and they all spent an uneasy night filled with long wakeful spells and restless dreams.

Morning came as a great relief. Somehow problems always look more manageable in the daylight than in the dark. And morning brought all the inmates together again. They had learned that there were solace and strength in being together.

While they were having breakfast in the dining room, the phone rang. They could hear the ring from the kitchen phone and the muffled ring of the phone in the office. Opal didn't move to answer it. Neither did anyone else.

It rang thirteen times before it stopped.

"Thirteen isn't a very lucky number," Lyle said, glancing nervously at Virgil.

The phone began to ring again. Somehow it seemed louder and more insistent this time. Again, it stopped after thirteen rings. Virgil and Lyle moved their chairs closer to each other and held each other's hands.

"I give them an hour, tops," Opal said. "I'll bet they don't even try the doorbell. They'll come right in."

"Why should they ring the doorbell?" Mr. Moreland asked. "They're sure there won't be anyone in here who could answer it."

"What are we going to do when they come?" Boom-Boom asked in a voice that was halfway between his little kid's voice and his grown-up one.

"We could play dead," Graham suggested. "And when they come into the library, we could all jump up and scare them out of their wits."

Boom-Boom giggled. "Yeah," he said. "That would be fun."

"I think it would be better if we pretend nothing has happened," Mr. Moreland said. "If we play dead, they'll know we're on to them. We want to keep them guessing. Let them think their canister of gas failed to work."

Forty-five minutes later they were in the library, with the door to the hall open, occupied with their usual activities, when the front door stealthily opened and Bart and Bernie stuck their heads cautiously in.

"Do you hear anything?" Bernie asked in a stage whisper.

"How can I hear anything with you hissing in my ear?" Bart answered, not bothering to lower his voice. "There won't be anything to hear, anyhow."

They closed the door and came across the hall to the library. Dr. Waldemar got out of his chair by the fire and walked to the door to meet them. "Is there something I can do for you?" he asked mildly.

The color drained from Bart's and Bernie's faces. Then Bernie's eyes rolled up into his head and he fell over backward. When his head hit the floor, the house shook a little and everyone in the library winced.

Bart opened his mouth but nothing came out.

Dr. Waldemar waited patiently for an answer to his question.

Finally Bart found his voice. "I . . . ," he croaked. "We just came by to see how our brother is."

"He's doing as well as can be expected," Dr. Waldemar said, sounding just like a real doctor, which he was, but it had been a long time since he'd had to sound like one. "But your other brother doesn't seem to be doing as well."

Bart glanced down at Bernie. "Oh, he gets these . . . spells. He'll be all right."

"Well, good-bye," Dr. Waldemar said. "Nice of you to stop by." He started back to his chair.

"Uh, you're all looking well," Bart said, still standing in the doorway.

"We are, thank you," Dr. Waldemar said.

"No flu or colds or any other ailments?" Bart asked.

"Nothing at all," Dr. Waldemar said. "We're all unusually healthy. Sometimes I think there's something in the air at Walnut Manor that protects us from ever getting sick. We'll probably live forever out here."

Bart muttered something under his breath.

"What was that?" Dr. Waldemar asked.

"Nothing," Bart said.

"I thought you said, 'Not if I can help it.' "

"Of course not," Bart said. "Why would I say such a thing?"

"I couldn't imagine. Do you want some help with your brother?"

"No." Bart grabbed Bernie by the leg and dragged him to the front door, which was still standing open, and right down the steps to their car.

When the sound of the car's engine faded into the distance, Everett said, " 'It's not death that a man should fear, but he should fear never beginning to live.' Marcus Aurelius. 121 to 180."

"Well, I feel more alive than I have for a long time," Mr. Moreland said. "I think Dr. Waldemar does, too." He clapped Dr. Waldemar on the shoulder. "Doc, your performance was fabulous. Nothing like a good crisis to make one feel alert and cheerful. Remember, L. Barlow, how it was when our companies were in trouble? Didn't you feel sharp witted and cunning then?"

Mr. Van Dyke nodded with fond remembrance.

"I feel that way again, don't you?" Mr. Moreland asked.

Mr. Van Dyke nodded again.

"We're going to get them," Mr. Moreland said. "I know we will."

"You better get those sharp wits to work in a hurry, then," Opal told him. "Those guys aren't going to wait long before they make another try. And sooner or later they'll succeed. We can't always be as lucky as we were yesterday."

"Wouldn't it be simplest to have Dr. Waldemar report the cooked books?" Sandy asked. "Even if he has been careless about his paperwork, surely the authorities would believe him."

"And then what do you think would happen?" Opal asked. "At the very least, Dr. Waldemar would lose his job for letting this criminal activity go on for so long. I probably would, too."

"According to these records," Mr. Moreland said, "there's no pension plan for either of you. Losing your jobs would leave you with no money and no place to live. Dr. Waldemar is too old to be looking for another job."

"And what do you think would happen to Walnut Manor?" Opal asked. "Except for Sandy's and Bentley's family, it's been years since we've had a new patient."

There was a long heavy silence as they all realized that if they blew the whistle on the board of directors, it would be the end of Walnut Manor. It surprised them to realize that they now felt about Walnut Manor the way Mole had felt about his cozy home. They couldn't imagine living anywhere else. And when they thought about where they might be sent if Walnut Manor closed, they all shuddered.

"What can we do?" Graham asked.

"There's got to be something," Mr. Moreland said, frowning. "There's got to be a way to get somebody to pay attention to the ravings of a bunch of nut cases who haven't been out in the real world for years. Somebody who would overlook Dr. Waldemar's inattention to business and Opal's . . . ah . . . eccentricities."

Mr. Van Dyke was shaking his head sadly, thinking of his son on the board.

Virgil and Lyle shook their heads, and so, finally, did Graham.

" 'Our repentance is not so much regret for the evil we have done, as fear of its consequences.' Duc de La Rochefoucauld. 1613 to 1680," Everett said.

"So we have to come up with some good consequences," Opal said. "Any ideas?"

For the rest of the day there was silence in the library as everyone thought. Just before five o'clock, Sandy went into the office and made a phone call.

CHAPTER

18

- - - - - - -

The next morning, when Sunnie opened the door to the sickroom to take in the breakfast trays, Louie, tired of being cooped up for so long, ran unnoticed past her and scampered down the stairs. He sauntered into the library and curled up in L. Barlow Van Dyke's unoccupied chair.

Sandy arrived, just as breakfast was over, and sat down at the table to join everyone in having an extra cup of coffee. Bentley was hot on the trail of another possible cure, so he had remained at Eclipse. After their coffee, they all helped Opal clear the table and wash the dishes. As Everett put the last dry dish away, Sandy said, "I have a plan. Why don't you come into the library and let me tell you about it."

They trooped into the library and took their customary seats, Mr. Van Dyke having to lift Louie onto his lap so he could sit down. Sandy stood by the fireplace. He'd gone over his plan with Bentley several times the night before, looking for flaws in it, but they hadn't found any. Now, looking out at the hopeful faces of the people he'd come to care so much about, he worried that his plan was too naive or implausible to work. After all, what did he know about the world?

As he opened his mouth to speak, Boom-Boom screamed, a high-pitched, frightened-child scream, and pointed to Louie in Mr. Van Dyke's lap. "He has Louie!" Boom-Boom cried. "And he's a cat molester!"

Louie, scared awake by Boom-Boom's scream, jumped up and climbed Mr. Van Dyke's chest until he was pressed under his chin with his paws around the man's neck. Mr. Van Dyke cuddled Louie against him protectively and, though bright red in the face, said with dignity, "I am not and never have been a cat molester."

Well, you could have heard a feather drop in the library then.

"Why didn't you say so sooner?" Opal finally asked irritably.

"I was too mad," Mr. Van Dyke said. "The first day I came here, or, rather, was brought here"—he stopped to clear his throat. His voice had a rusty, unused quality about it—"against my wishes, I should add, you asked me what I would like to be called. I told you, but you thought I'd said 'Cat molester,' and you told everyone to be careful with cats around me. I was so insulted. I, L. Barlow Van Dyke,"—he cleared his throat again— "a man of wealth and culture being referred to as a common cat molester. It was intolerable. I've always had a hot temper. My explosions, in fact, were one of the reasons my family put me in here, I suppose. I was determined not to lose my temper the minute I arrived; I figured that would only make things worse for me. So I thought I'd keep quiet until I got over being mad, and, well, at first it was kind of restful, and then it just got to be a habit."

"What *did* you want to be called?" Lyle asked.

Mr. Van Dyke cleared his throat again, but already his voice was much stronger and surer. "You know how I always wear this yachting cap? That's because I like to think of myself as captain of my fate. It's a sad joke, considering where I've ended up, but I still like wearing the cap. And my first name is Lester. So I wanted to be called Captain Lester."

"Captain Lester?" Boom-Boom said. "Oh, I get it! If you say it fast it *does* sound like 'cat molester.' Well, gee whiz, I don't see what the fuss was all about."

Mr. Van Dyke looked abashed. "It does seem silly now. But I must have been more . . . distressed when I arrived than I realized. The way all of us were."

"But aren't anymore," Sandy said. "Except for poor Eddy. I can't say I've really seen any improvement in him. But that's what my plan is all about. You know, Mr. Moreland, how you said nobody would listen to us because we're all a bunch of nuts—or incompetent, in my case. Well, I don't think we are anymore. So last night I called our family doctor, Dr. Malcolm, and asked him to come out to Walnut Manor with a colleague of his to examine all of us and certify us as sound in mind and body. *Then* we can bring our charges against the board and no one can dispute us.

At least, not on those grounds." He paused and then went on. "And just because I'm so sure we're really all right, last night I faxed all the incriminating papers to the Senior Partner among all of Horatio's lawyers."

He waited, breathless, for someone to tell him his plan was poppycock.

"Wiener schnitzel!" Mr. Moreland cried. "That's genius! Then what?"

"Well, I have another idea, too," Sandy said. "You'd better tell me if it will work."

Just then they heard Sunnie yelling from upstairs. "Louie's missing! Is he anywhere near Mr. Van Dyke?"

Boom-Boom ran across the hall to the foot of the stairs and yelled up, "He's in his lap. And he's fine. Mr. Van Dyke isn't a cat molester after all. He's just Captain Lester."

"I don't know what that means," Sunnie called down, "but I'm sure somebody will explain it to me eventually." She paused. "Is everything all right down there?"

"We're fine," Boom-Boom yelled. "Sandy has an idea. I can't keep yelling up the stairs, it hurts my throat. We'll tell you later."

"All right," Sunnie said, and those two words sounded so lonely and disappointed and left out that everyone in the library got up in one movement (except for Dr. Waldemar who had to be awakened and Eddy who had to be carried) and went upstairs to the sickroom.

There, Sandy explained his idea again—the one that

Mr. Moreland had said was genius—and hoped he didn't look as proud and flattered as he felt. And then he explained his other idea.

Mr. Moreland was at a loss for words. He had already used up *genius* on the previous idea, and this one was so much better that he didn't know *what* to call it. Sunnie got her thesaurus out, and Mr. Moreland finally decided on *original, creative,* and *inventive.*

Sandy was thrilled by this praise, and even more thrilled that Mr. Moreland and Captain Lester thought his second idea would work like a charm. But what he was waiting for was Sunnie's response. She said she loved the idea better than anything she had ever heard, but she still didn't look directly at him. Sandy wished he didn't care as much as he did.

"We've still got a couple of problems," Opal said, bringing everyone down to earth with a thump. "One, Bart and Bernie are still trying to kill us, and two, our sleepers are still asleep. No matter how terrific Sandy's ideas are, they won't change those things."

For the rest of the day, the inmates seesawed between elation about Sandy's ideas and deep discouragement about Opal's. It gave them an inkling of what it must have felt like to be Boom-Boom as he changed back and forth from child to adult.

Bentley told them at dinnertime that he was getting close to a cure he thought had promise, and he told them he had analyzed the Pensa-Cola canister and had found no traces of Pensa-Cola syrup. In fact, no traces of anything. So the canister had either been delivered pristinely empty, which was unlikely, or it had contained something so volatile and evaporative, the way cyanosulfidioxinethonoxide was, that it had been *left* pristinely empty when the gas was gone.

After a subdued dinner and a chapter of *Treasure Island*, they all went to bed. They needed a good night's sleep to be fresh for tomorrow, when Dr. Malcolm and his colleague Dr. Trinidad, the brilliant, world-famous psychiatrist, were coming to examine them.

There is no more dependable way to ensure a restless night than to convince oneself that a good night's sleep is absolutely essential. Consequently, by the next morning, they were all gritty eyed and crabby from insufficient sleep.

Dr. Malcolm and Dr. Trinidad, a regal dark-skinned woman with a melodic foreign accent, arrived right after breakfast and set to work.

It took them all day, but they finally got everyone examined, and promised to deliver the results of all the tests in two days. That day was also when the meeting with Horatio's lawyers was scheduled, to get started on Sandy's second idea, as well as to decide what to do about the board of directors.

Sandy invited the doctors to stay for dinner, but they declined. Dr. Malcolm whispered to Sandy as he left, "I've never spent a whole day with worse-tempered people. Are they always so peevish?"

"Just Opal. She's worse lately because she's quit

smoking. But the rest of us were all so nervous, we couldn't sleep last night and it's made us grouchy. I hope it won't influence our tests."

"If grouchiness were an illness, there wouldn't be a soul on the streets; we'd all be in hospitals," Dr. Malcolm assured him. "But I hope you understand if we don't want to stay for dinner."

"Of course," Sandy said. "I can't say I'm looking forward to it myself."

It was a good thing Dr. Malcolm and Dr. Trinidad hadn't stayed for dinner: It was awful. Boom-Boom spilled his milk, and burst into tears when Opal scolded him more severely than was necessary. When Mr. Moreland told her so, she told him to mind his own business, *if* he could remember what it was. When Captain Lester came to Mr. Moreland's defense, Opal said she liked it better when he couldn't talk. Graham, Virgil, and Lyle were smart enough to keep their mouths shut, but their faces were rebellious and stormy. Everett muttered to himself.

Sandy wished he were upstairs in the peaceful sickroom with Sunnie and his parents. He wished he were at Eclipse with Bentley, who was so hard at work on his cure that he'd decided to skip dinner. He wished he were anyplace but where he was, and he began to wonder if his second idea was such a good one after all.

The next morning, after a night in which they all slept as if they'd been hit in the head with a club, they were their old selves again. Opal apologized to Mr.

Moreland by saying she knew he remembered enough of his own business to mind it, and to Captain Lester by telling him that she was glad he could talk again and that eventually he might say something she wanted to listen to. To Boom-Boom she simply said she was sorry.

Sandy's sleep had been disturbed at Eclipse by the sounds of Bentley prowling through the house. As far as Sandy knew, Bentley had been up most of the night, though when Sandy was ready to go to Walnut Manor, he found Bentley sprawled on the floor of the laboratory, sound asleep.

Sandy bicycled to Walnut Manor, leaving the Daimler for Bentley in case he woke up in time for lunch.

But lunchtime came and went with no Bentley. He'd never stayed away from Walnut Manor and Flossie for so long, and Sandy began to worry.

The other inmates, Opal, and Dr. Waldemar headed outside for exercise, leaving Sandy, Mr. Moreland, and Captain Lester at the card table working on their plans, and Eddy lying by the fireplace.

The front door burst open so violently, it hit the wall and bounced closed again.

Sandy, Mr. Moreland, and Captain Lester jumped to their feet. Captain Lester grabbed the fireplace poker and Sandy grabbed the ash shovel. Mr. Moreland was left with only the little hearth broom for protection.

The door opened more slowly this time, and Bentley came through it holding a jar filled with a black substance. Bentley's hair and clothes were disheveled, he had bags under his eyes, and his shoelaces were untied.

Relieved, Sandy, Mr. Moreland, and Captain Lester put down their weapons. "What happened to you, man?" Mr. Moreland asked. "You look a wreck."

"I feel a wreck," Bentley said. There was a wild light in his eyes, and Sandy wondered if all the work and the worry of the past months had driven him over the edge. "But I've got something"—he waved the jar—"that I think, I hope, might do it."

Sandy wanted to feel hopeful, the way he had with each of Bentley's other cures, but he had been disappointed too many times.

"That stuff looks horrible," Sandy said. "Are you sure it's safe to give to the sleepers?"

"I took some myself," Bentley said. "As you can see, what it's done is make me more alert."

Sandy wasn't sure that's how he'd have described Bentley's condition. Mr. Moreland and Captain Lester looked unconvinced, as well.

"Maybe you'd like some lunch first," Sandy suggested. "Sit down and rest a while."

"No!" Bentley almost screamed. "I must try this immediately. Immediately!"

Sandy sometimes felt frantic and furious at the lack of a cure. He sometimes wanted to yell and curse about it. But he never got the way Bentley was today.

Bentley ran across the hallway and started up the stairs, stumbling on his untied shoelaces. With Sandy, Mr. Moreland, and Captain Lester right behind him, he ran to the sickroom and threw open the door, startling Sunnie so much that she dropped her book on seventeenth-century architecture.

"What's wrong?" she said, jumping to her feet. "Is it Bart and Bernie?"

"No," Sandy said, "it's Bentley."

"I *know* that's Bentley," Sunnie said crossly. "I meant, are you all upset because of Bart and Bernie."

Sandy was speechless. He'd never heard Sunnie sound cross, not in all the time he'd known her. It made sense that she should be sometimes. Everybody was. But it was such a shock to see Sunnie—who'd always lived up to her name—acting like Opal, that Sandy didn't know what to say.

While he stood there staring at her, he realized that she was staring back at him. He felt a little dizzy and strange as he looked, at last, into her big blue eyes. He forgot there was anything else in the room to look at. Something was happening, something that felt the way the air does before lightning strikes, when the hair on your arms and on your head lifts and there's a fizzy energy all around you. He didn't know what it was or what would happen next. All he knew was he couldn't look away, and neither, apparently, could she.

While they stood, eyes locked, Bentley filled an eye-dropper with the viscous black stuff and forced it into Attila's beak. Mr. Moreland and Captain Lester wrung their hands and frowned and looked uncomfortably at each other. While they both knew that sometimes extremely important events were totally beyond their control, and that sometimes the best course of action was simply to stand aside and do nothing, they didn't really believe it.

Bentley massaged Attila's throat to get her to swallow, and she grimaced in her sleep. She still wore the sweater Opal had knitted for her. She looked pretty mangy, though her feathers were growing back in.

"Must taste about as bad as it looks," Captain Lester said uneasily.

Bentley had just laid Attila back down on her bed of towels when they heard a rusty sound, like the hinges of an old gate opening.

Bentley bent over the dishpan, listening. "It's Attila!" he exclaimed. "She's making a sound."

"She made one before," Mr. Moreland reminded him. "Hiccups."

The rusty sound continued.

"That's how my throat felt," Captain Lester said, "when I started talking again. Rusty and scratchy."

The rusty sound changed into a faint but recognizable cluck.

A second after the sound of the cluck, Louie came tearing into the room from Captain Lester's chair in the library. He climbed up Bentley as if he were a telephone pole and jumped from his shoulder into the dishpan, where he began licking Attila's face. Attila's eyes opened.

Bentley burst into tears for the second time in a week; for the second time since he was a little boy.

Mr. Moreland and Captain Lester looked at each

other, openmouthed. "I'll be double dampened," Mr. Moreland said reverently.

"Me, too," Captain Lester agreed.

"Hey, Sandy," Mr. Moreland said, passing his hand between Sandy and Sunnie, who both had missed everything happening with Attila because they were still staring into each other's eyes. "Pay attention."

Sandy blinked as if he were waking up from a beautiful and complicated dream. "What?" he asked.

"Look at Attila."

Sandy looked. "Oh, my gosh. She's awake!" He put his arms around Bentley as he wept, and patted him on the back. "You did it, Bentley, you did it. I'm sorry I ever doubted you."

"I didn't know you were doubting me," Bentley sobbed. "I thought I was doing enough doubting for all of us."

Sandy kept patting Bentley's back. "So what are you waiting for? Give it to Horatio and Mousey and Flossie."

"I'm afraid," Bentley cried. "Just because it works on a chicken doesn't mean it'll work on people. What if it has a bad effect? I could never forgive myself."

"Just give them the amount you gave yourself. It didn't hurt you. It just made you more, more . . ."

"I know. More everything. Maybe you're right. Maybe I could." He straightened up and searched for his handkerchief.

Before he could find it, Sunnie handed him hers, already wet with her own tears. "Go ahead, Bentley,"

Sunnie said. "What is life without risks? How could our sleepers be worse off than they already are?"

"Oh, they could be," Bentley said, blowing his nose loudly.

"Oh, that," Sunnie conceded. "Well, sure, they could die. But maybe that would be preferable to the way they are now. It would be to me."

"If it doesn't work on humans . . ." Bentley said, sniffing, "at least we know we have a drug that brings chickens out of comas."

Bentley anxiously prepared three more doses of the ugly black stuff and gave them to Horatio, Mousey, and Flossie.

"Should we call the others in?" Sandy asked. "Just in case?"

"Let's wait," Bentley said. "Just in case."

Then Bentley, Sandy, Sunnie, Mr. Moreland, and Captain Lester stood at the foot of the sleepers' beds, waiting.

Nothing happened. They stood waiting for twenty minutes more, and still nothing happened.

By this time Attila appeared to be fully recovered, running under the beds, frolicking with Louie, clucking, and pecking at the flowers on the carpet as if nothing had ever been wrong with her.

Sunnie, Sandy, Mr. Moreland, Captain Lester, and Bentley pulled chairs up around the beds to wait as the minutes became hours. One by one the other inmates, Opal, and Dr. Waldemar came in from outside and joined them in the sickroom.

Sunnie sat by Mousey's bed holding her hand and talking to her in a low voice. "Please wake up. I've looked forward for so long to getting to know you. I bet you've got some good stories you could tell me, and I could tell you a lot about whales and gemstones and seventeenth-century architecture, and a little bit about financial planning. Oh, please wake up."

As Sunnie spoke, Mousey's eyelids fluttered open. "Fleur," she murmured in a smooth and mellifluous voice. "Fleur LaRoche, my dear old friend. What are you doing here?"

Sunnie stared at her. "Fleur LaRoche? How did you know about her?"

"Don't you remember?" Mousey asked, sitting up. "It was a long time ago, but don't you remember *Social Service*?"

Sandy couldn't contain himself. He forgot everything his parents had taught him about not interrupting a conversation and grabbed his mother in his arms. "Mousey! How do you feel? What's happened to your voice?"

"I feel just fine, dear," she said. "What are you so excited about?" She looked around her. "Where am I?" she asked, beginning to look frightened. "What's wrong with Horatio? And Flossie? Who are all these people?"

Just then Horatio and Flossie opened their eyes and sat up.

Bentley burst into tears *again* and threw himself across Flossie's lap while all the inmates cheered and whistled and stomped their feet on the floor. Louie and Attila hid under Mousey's bed.

Horatio took one look around and scrunched down into his bed, pulling the covers over his head. Flossie sat up, clutching the blankets under her chin with one hand and stroking the sobbing Bentley with the other while she gazed around her with eyes as big as dinner plates.

19

It was past suppertime before all the explanations had been made and before the sleepers—now wakers— learned what had happened while they slept. Opal ran between the sickroom—now the wellroom—and the kitchen, trying to get dinner started and be in on all the excitement, too. Finally she gave up, sat down on the floor next to Flossie's bed, and said, "The heck with it. We'll send out for pizza. I haven't had a day off in years."

The pizza came eventually and it was as cold as Bart's and Bernie's hearts when it arrived, for it was a long way to Jupiter. But Opal warmed it up again, and the wakers put on their bathrobes and slippers and came downstairs to eat in the dining room with everyone else.

During dinner Mousey said to Sunnie, "I can see now you aren't my old friend Fleur LaRoche, but you sound just like her, and there is a little something in your face that reminds me of her."

"Dear Mousey," Sunnie said. "How could you know? Fleur LaRoche was my mother. That was her stage name. Her real name was Iris Stone. She used to reminisce so much about her happy days on the stage with her friends. I've often wondered if you were the Mousey she remembered so fondly—after all, how many Mouseys do you meet in a lifetime?—but I couldn't ask you, of course. Oh, I could have asked you, but you couldn't have answered. That was the real problem. Anyway, I hoped it was you. My poor mother has passed on now, but I still have her scrapbooks. I hope you and I will have a chance to look at them some-time."

"That would be lovely, Sunnie. I look forward to it. When I was asleep I dreamed of a blond angel talking to me, but I never thought I'd actually get to meet her."

"Oh, I must apologize to you for something I said while you were asleep. Remember how I promised you a steak and a hug when you woke up? Now you're awake, and what you got was pizza and no hug. I don't usually do that, not keep a promise. I think promises are very important and I take them seriously. I just didn't know when you were going to wake up, and it's hard to plan for a steak dinner when things go the way they did this afternoon. How about steak for dinner tomorrow night?"

"Steak tomorrow will be fine," Mousey said. "But I'd like the hug right now."

And she got it.

Something had been bothering Sandy ever since

Mousey had uttered her first words. "Mousey," he said as soon as he could get a word in edgewise, what with all the explanations and introductions. "Have you noticed how different your voice is since you woke up?"

"Why, you're right. I must have forgotten what I sounded like before. Do you suppose all my vocal cords needed was a nice long rest to work right?"

"I don't know," Sandy said, "but I can't get used to the way you sound. Like a completely different person."

"Maybe I am different now," Mousey said. "Something like this has to have an effect on one, don't you think?"

"I don't care what you sound like," Horatio said. "You're still my beautiful Mousey, and I couldn't love you any more than I do at this moment, when we've been returned to each other."

"Oh, Horatio," Mousey said, "you know I feel exactly the same way about you. I'm positive it was a comfort to me while I was asleep to know that you were right there beside me."

Opal got up abruptly from the table, taking a couple of empty pizza boxes with her out to the kitchen.

Mr. Moreland got up, too, and followed her.

"Well, now we've got only one more problem to solve," Boom-Boom said. "Bart and Bernie."

"I'm sure we'll find a way," Sunnie said, though for once she didn't sound as convincingly optimistic as she usually did. Bart and Bernie, for all their lumpishness and stolidity, had turned out to be tenacious adversaries.

Bentley and Flossie decided to go back to Eclipse for the night. Bentley wanted to be alone with her while his galloping emotions settled down, and Flossie was having similar sentiments. Besides, all her clothes were at Eclipse and she was tired, she said, of wearing pajamas.

But Mousey and Horatio were having such a good time with their new friends that they decided to spend one more night at Walnut Manor, and they insisted that Sandy stay on with them.

When Bentley and Flossie got ready to leave, promising to bring changes of clothes for Horatio, Mousey, and Sandy first thing the next morning, Opal and Mr. Moreland came out of the kitchen to say good-bye. They both had odd looks on their faces, looks that were completely new to both of them.

"Why do you look so funny?" Boom-Boom asked them.

"You think I look funny?" Opal asked.

"Not like that," Boom-Boom said hastily. "I mean, you just look different. A way I've never seen you look. Mr. Moreland, too."

"Shall we tell them, Opal?" Mr. Moreland asked her.

Amazingly, she blushed, lowered her eyes, and nodded.

"Opal and I are going to get married," Mr. Moreland announced.

There was the same kind of silence there'd been the day Captain Lester spoke for the first time.

"Well . . . schnauzer!" Captain Lester finally said.

He grabbed Mr. Moreland's hand and shook it heartily. "Congratulations, Whit. I think you've found yourself a bride who can keep you in line."

Mr. Moreland laughed uproariously, a way no one had ever heard him laugh before, which showed how happy he was. "I think you're right about that, Captain. I've always liked a spirited woman—just never found one with *enough* spirit. Until now. When I saw the way Horatio and Mousey looked at each other at dinner, it made me think. Then I looked up and saw Opal carrying those pizza boxes and realized . . . well, I wasn't totally out of my mind that day I pinched her." What could be seen of his cheeks around his beard were as flushed as Opal's.

Captain Lester kissed Opal in a brotherly way, and by then everybody else had recovered sufficiently from their surprise to offer their own best wishes. Sandy felt a curious ache in his heart as he shook Mr. Moreland's hand and hugged Opal.

"The wedding will be here, at Walnut Manor, as soon as we've got the details worked out," Mr. Moreland said. "And we want you *all* to be our attendants. It would be impossible to decide who should be the best man or the maid of honor."

Bentley and Flossie ran to the Daimler, raced to Eclipse for some champagne, and brought it back to Walnut Manor for a toast before they all staggered off, exhausted from a day full of so much tension and emotion, to their beds.

Sandy had thought he would sleep like a bear in hibernation, but he woke up suddenly in the middle of the night, eyes wide and alert. For a moment he was disoriented, until he realized that he was sleeping at Walnut Manor in the bed that had been Flossie's and not in his own bed at Eclipse. The clock on the bedside table said 3:03. He could hear Horatio and Mousey nearby, breathing deeply in their sleep, and he sent a grateful prayer of thanks to Bentley for assuring that they would wake from *this* night's sleep.

He was sure something had awakened him, but he didn't know what it was. The house was silent. There was no movement in the room. Raising up on his elbow, he saw that Louie and Attila were curled cozily together in the dishpan, sound asleep.

But something was tickling his nose. Something familiar, something he could almost identify. It was . . . it was . . . smoke! And smoke meant—

He leaped from his bed into his slippers and grabbed his robe. "Fire!" he yelled, shaking Horatio and then Mousey. "Fire! Wake up!"

As Horatio and Mousey sat up groggily, Sandy ran to the small adjoining bedroom that was Sunnie's. He couldn't help himself, he had to stop for just a millisecond to look at her as she slept, her halo of blond hair spread on the pillow, her face so sweet and peaceful in repose.

But this was an emergency and there was no time for admiring the woman he . . . never mind what he felt about her. He had to wake her up.

"Sunnie," he said urgently but softly, not wanting to scare her. It hadn't bothered him at all to shake his parents suddenly awake, but this was different somehow. "Sunnie," he said a little louder, and she opened her eyes.

"Hi," she said sleepily, looking directly into his eyes in the same way she had just before the sleepers awakened. "What is it?"

"I think the house is on fire," he said gently.

She sat straight up, her nurse's training at responding to emergencies coming immediately to the fore. "We've got to wake everybody up," she said, getting out of bed.

Sandy turned his head while Sunnie put on her robe.

"Do you think it's another of Bart and Bernie's plots?" she asked, hurrying out of the room behind him.

"I wouldn't be surprised in the least," he said, picking up the dishpan with Attila and Louie in it. "You call the fire department in Jupiter while I wake everyone and get them out of here."

A few minutes later all the inmates were gathered in the driveway in front of Walnut Manor, helplessly watching flames shoot from the roof. They hugged themselves and each other and shivered, not entirely from the cold.

Boom-Boom sucked his thumb and, with tears rolling down his face, clutched Sunnie's robe. Captain Lester held Louie under one arm and Attila under the other, and murmured comforting words to them as he watched the flames. Everett went from person to person telling them, " 'Adversity reveals genius, prosperity conceals it.' Horace. 65 to 8 B.C."

"I could give Horace an argument on that one," Mr. Moreland said, huddling with Opal for warmth.

It seemed a long time before the fire engines arrived, but once they did, the firefighters were able to extinguish the blaze quickly. And what did they find, as they searched over the house to make sure all the hot spots were out, but Bart and Bernie, crouched on the last unburned section of the roof.

The fire chief hauled them down, scorched and waterlogged. When the fire chief got to the bottom of the ladder, holding each of them by the scruff of his sopping overcoat, he asked, "Does anybody know who these guys are?"

Bart and Bernie took one look at Horatio and Mousey, who were looking back at them with equal amazement, and Bernie keeled over in a dead faint into the muddy and flowerless flower bed. Bart jerked his overcoat out of the fire chief's grip and started running down the driveway toward the road. A quick-thinking firefighter turned a high-pressure hose on him and knocked him flat.

It took a while for the fire chief to understand who Bart and Bernie were, what with everyone talking at once trying to tell him all the awful things the two had done. But when he understood what they were probably doing on the roof, he locked both Bart and Bernie in his car. Then he used the phone in one of the fire trucks to call the police.

"Stupidest arsonists I ever saw," he said. "They climbed up a ladder next to the chimney—wanted to make it look as if a spark from the fireplace had started the fire, I suppose—but the first thing that caught fire was the top of their ladder. Then they were stuck on the roof—too cowardly to jump and too stupid to climb down the trellis on the other side."

Bart pressed his fat face against the window of the fire chief's car and shouted, "Trellis? There was a trellis? We're victims of circumstantial evidence! We were looking for shooting stars! This is the clearest night of the year! We had nothing to do with any fire!"

CHAPTER

20

The police arrived and spent almost an hour trying to get statements about Bart and Bernie from all the residents of Walnut Manor. Aside from the fact that everybody except Eddy wanted to talk at the same time, the stories seemed simply too preposterous to be believed: poisoned birthday cake and a comatose chicken; Pensa-Cola canisters full of disappearing gas and attempts to freeze a houseful of people. There was also something about games of Investment, whatever that was, and snow people and *The Wind in the Willows*. At the same time a muscular young man kept trying to lift up one end of a fire engine. Finally the police threw up their hands and said they'd come back the next day when everyone was more rested and their lips weren't blue with cold. They promised to keep Bart and Bernie locked up until a clear story and some reasonable charges emerged.

The firefighters gave the residents of Walnut Manor

a ride to Eclipse in their fire trucks. This cheered Boom-Boom up quite a bit and frightened Virgil and Lyle, until it was over and then they felt extremely proud of themselves—especially when Mr. Moreland, Captain Lester, and Horatio, all of whom had done so many exciting and important things in their lives, told them that this was the first time *they* had ever ridden in a fire engine, too.

Naturally Bentley and Flossie were surprised to see them all, in their nightclothes, in the middle of the night, but as soon as they learned what had happened, they made sandwiches and coffee and beds. As it turned out, no one ever actually got to bed again that night. By the time they had calmed down enough to sleep, it was broad daylight, and Horatio's lawyers had to be called to come to Eclipse instead of to Walnut Manor, as did Dr. Malcolm and Dr. Trinidad. The insurance adjusters had to be notified about the fire, and so did the board of directors, the cause of so many problems.

The doctors and lawyers arrived first, luckily, and by the time the insurance adjusters showed up, the necessary legal papers had been signed and the most important arrangements for the future had been made.

Dr. Malcolm and Dr. Trinidad had examined Horatio and Mousey and Flossie. Though they would have to wait for the test results, from what the doctors could tell, none of the three had suffered any ill effects at all. They seemed as fresh and as rested as if they had just returned from a long vacation.

When the insurance adjusters arrived, everyone went back to Walnut Manor with them to look at the destruction and see what could be salvaged.

Poor Walnut Manor was a mess. The actual fire damage was restricted to the roof and the attics, but the water from the fire hoses had flooded down through the entire house and almost everything inside was soaked and ruined. The beautiful parquetry floors that Opal had kept so highly polished with her skate mops had peeled and buckled, the wallpaper hung in soggy shreds, the carpets squished and squelched when trod upon, Sunnie's books and all the books in the library were sopping and had already begun to mildew. Virgil and Lyle sadly stroked the short-circuited television set that would never again broadcast *Bowling for Dollars*.

The only thing that had survived without damage was the locked metal file cabinet in the library, full of documents that revealed, without meaning to, how the board of directors had been embezzling Walnut Manor's money for so many years.

"Graham," Mr. Moreland said, "I think it would be a good idea for you to take that file cabinet out to the Daimler. We'd better keep it at Eclipse until this is all settled."

Old Dr. Waldemar was quite overcome to see the place he had loved too much to leave—even when he could barely keep it going—in such a sorry state. He had to go out onto the front porch and sit on the top step with his head between his knees to keep from getting sick. Graham wheeled Eddy out onto the porch to keep Dr. Waldemar company, and slowly the rest of them assembled around him, as sick at heart, if not at stomach, as he. He had done his best—even when his powers had begun to fail him—to take care of those for whom he was responsible. He had loved his work and his charges, and had been ingenious in caring for them in the face of dwindling resources, increasing age and isolation, and an unscrupulous board of directors. Such dedication, love, and loyalty were not common qualities anymore, especially in the business world.

Now Dr. Waldemar's vocation, avocation, and home were all gone at once. He had every right to feel sad and sick. And none of his friends could see him suffer without suffering themselves. Especially when they had their own reasons to be sad.

" 'If you suffer, thank God!—it is a sure sign that you are alive.' " Everett finally said. "Elbert Hubbard." He stood up and walked down the steps to the Daimler.

"He's right," Sunnie said, who had had surprisingly little to say about all the events of the past twenty-four hours. "We should think about how lucky we are to have one another, and how lucky it is that none of us was injured in the fire. We should think about how happy we are that Mousey and Flossie and Horatio and Attila are awake and fine, and that we have Eclipse right next door. We should think about the satisfaction we'll feel when Bart and Bernie are locked up for good. And now we should go back to Eclipse because the police will be arriving soon, and after them, the board of directors. And *that* revenge is going to be absolutely delicious, isn't it?"

Bentley and Sandy took turns ferrying them all back to Eclipse in time to talk with the police again. This interview wasn't much more organized than the one conducted in the middle of the night in the driveway in front of Walnut Manor, but eventually a somewhat coherent story emerged, and multiple charges of attempted murder were made against Bart and Bernie.

Then, to everyone's dismay, both Horatio's lawyers and the police said they were doubtful that the charges could be made to stick. There was simply no evidence. No poisoned birthday cake, no traces of poison gas in the Pensa-Cola canister, no identified cohort in the phone company or the utility company to prove the power had been deliberately shut off, no identified person who had delivered the suspicious Pensa-Cola canister, only circumstantial evidence of arson.

"But if you let them go, they'll keep trying until they do us all in," Boom-Boom cried. "They may start going after us one or two at a time, instead of all at once. We'll be run over or kidnapped or electrocuted in the bathtub or *something,* but they'll get us. They may be stupid, but they're persistent."

"I'm sorry," the police lieutenant said. "We can't continue to hold them without evidence. It violates their constitutional rights."

"What about our constitutional rights?" Captain Lester demanded.

" 'Life, liberty, and the pursuit of happiness,' " Everett said. "The preamble to the Constitution of the United States of America."

"Especially the *life* part," Virgil said softly.

"The lieutenant's right," one of the lawyers said.

And they all sat in the living room at Eclipse, shaking their heads and feeling furious and helpless and frightened.

Suddenly Bentley jumped to his feet and rushed from the room.

When he returned he was carrying a brown paper sack that looked as if it contained something heavy. He thrust the sack into the police lieutenant's hands. "Here," he said. "Here's your evidence."

The lieutenant opened the sack and looked inside. "It looks like a bottle of wine," she said.

"Not just wine," Bentley told her. "It's port." He shuddered slightly. "And not just port, but a particularly inferior vintage from a particularly bad year."

"I don't get it," the lieutenant said.

"I'm willing to bet," Bentley said, "that you'll find poison in that bottle, probably of some kind that simulates heart attacks or something of the sort. Furthermore, I think you'll find Bart's and Bernie's fingerprints all over that bottle. Not just on the outside, which would be perfectly logical since they're the ones who brought that bottle to Eclipse, but also underneath the lead covering on the cork, and probably even on the cork itself. Which would prove, wouldn't it, that they had tampered with the cork and the port and then gone to a lot of trouble to make it look as if the bottle were just an ordinary bottle of wine. So ordinary that an unsuspecting person might just drink a glass of it. Which would probably be the last glass of anything he ever drank in his life."

"Yeah?" the lieutenant said, getting interested. "Well, we'd better have this port analyzed. If what you think turns out to be true, your case would be a lot stronger. We'd have something to hang the rest of the circumstantial evidence on. Right?" she said, turning to the Senior Partner of all the lawyers.

"Right," the Senior Partner said. "And you can trust us to work as hard as we can to pin this on Bart and Bernie. We have no doubt they've done everything you say and, probably, more. After all, we've dealt with them for years. We know what they're capable of."

Bentley rode with the police lieutenant to the front gate to open it for the police to leave. The lawyers were staying on for the next event. Before he could close the gate behind the police cruisers, the cars bearing the board of directors began to arrive.

Bentley jogged back to the house. He didn't want to miss anything about this meeting of the board of directors with the lawyers and with the relatives they weren't expecting to see.

When Bentley reached Eclipse's front door, a line of shiny new cars had already parked along the curb and a group of well-dressed people was entering the house. Bentley followed them into the living room.

The Senior Partner, the rest of the lawyers, the insurance people, the residents of Walnut Manor, Dr. Waldemar, Opal, Sunnie, Sandy, Flossie, Horatio, and Mousey were already seated and waiting. Louie and Attila, oblivious to the tension in the air, wrestled joyfully in the middle of the floor, happy to be back to their old games.

The Senior Partner indicated chairs for the board of directors, who looked surprised to find so many people waiting for them. As soon as they were seated, the Senior Partner began to speak. "What's been going on at Walnut Manor in the past few months is too complicated to get into right now," she said, "though, if you were a proper board of directors, doing what a board of directors should be doing instead of merely using Walnut Manor as a source of unreported income, you would already know."

There were several outraged gasps and some indignant exclamations from the board, but the Senior Partner held up her hand for silence and continued. "It's too late for outrage and indignation. We have all the proof we need right here," and she patted the file cabinet affectionately. "Now, before we move ahead with criminal charges against all of you for the financial crimes you've committed, we have a proposition to offer you. I've said nothing about the moral crimes you've all committed—not only of abandoning your relatives at Walnut Manor, when all most of them needed were extra doses of love and understanding, but of then depriving them of the means to assure their comfort in order to give yourselves gain. I'd prefer not to say what I think of people who would do such a thing, since I tend to lose my temper.

"To recapitulate: We are aware of your crimes, both moral and criminal. We have proof of both kinds. We can go ahead and bring charges, thereby ruining you. Or you can accept the offer I'm about to make to you, in which case you will escape with some shreds of your reputations intact and my clients will get everything they want, which I think they are unquestionably entitled to, considering the way you've treated them over the years."

A man stood up and, red faced, sputtered, "We have no idea what you're talking about. I'm going to call my lawyer."

The Senior Partner, who had been holding a sheaf of papers, came up to the man and shoved the papers under his nose. "Look at these figures, here and here and here," she said, poking with her finger and shuffling the papers around. "I've had six accountants look at these figures, and they all say the same thing: embezzlement. Go ahead and call your lawyer."

The man sat down.

Across the room, Graham waved to him. "Hi, Dad," he said.

"What?" the man said. "Who are you?"

"It's Graham," Graham said. He stood up and held out his arms. "See?"

The man looked at his tall, muscular son. "You can't be. You don't look the slightest bit like Graham.

What's going on here? Is this some kind of a cult or something? Are we being brainwashed?"

"I assure you this is no cult," the Senior Partner said, "though I'm sure all of your brains could stand a good washing. And I assure you that that young man is your son Graham. He's one example of what love and care can accomplish. Now, here's our offer: We want you all to resign from the board of directors, and we want you to give back all the money you've embezzled over the years, with interest. We can work out a plan so you don't have to pay it back all at once, but you do have to pay it back. We want the deed of Walnut Manor transferred into the name of the Walnut Foundation, and we want you to pay for any repairs to Walnut Manor that the insurance company doesn't cover."

There was a stunned silence as the board contemplated just how much money they *had* embezzled over the years and what paying it back would mean to the ways they liked to live. Then they thought about how they would be living if they didn't pay the money back, and, suddenly, genteel poverty sounded pretty good—better than barred windows and black-and-white striped suits, anyway.

"We need to talk about this," Graham's father said.

The Senior Partner showed the board into the dining room and closed the doors. The instant she did, there was an explosion of voices from behind the doors, though none of the words were intelligible. It was probably just as well.

Sunnie, who was sitting next to Graham, patted his shoulder and said, "You must have felt terrible when your own father didn't recognize you."

"No," Graham said. "I didn't feel terrible at all. It was wonderful to know I've changed so much. I don't ever want him to recognize me again."

"I don't think any of our relatives recognized us," Captain Lester said. "It's as if we don't even exist for them anymore. And not one of them asked what would happen to us when Walnut Manor passed from their control."

"Who do you suppose they think we are?" Lyle asked.

Captain Lester shrugged. "Lawyers. Insurance people. Members of Horatio and Mousey's family. Who cares? We're not members of our old families anymore, that's for sure."

"Well, you *are* members of our family now," Mousey said in her new voice. "We're all members of the Walnut Foundation family."

"Wait'll they hear what we have in mind for the Walnut Foundation," Boom-Boom said gleefully. "They're going to freak!"

The doors to the dining room sprang open, and the board trooped silently back to their seats, their faces a compendium of resignation, displeasure, and fear.

"We accept your terms," Graham's father said, after the others had sat down. "As if we have a choice." Then he sat down, too. "The only question we have is, what's the Walnut Foundation?"

The Senior Partner smiled and said, "The Walnut Foundation is the brainstorm of Horatio's son, Sandy, who is as brilliant as his father. He's also the one who figured out the embezzlement payback plan. The Walnut Foundation will be a nonprofit organization dedicated to helping people who are too frazzled by modern life to find the balance they need between work and play. The wall will come down between Eclipse and Walnut Manor, and both mansions will be part of the campus. People will apply to come, free of charge, for a visit of anywhere from a week to a couple of months—however long it takes them to get detoxified from the rat race, reorganize their priorities, and feel ready to leave. They do have to leave. It's not any healthier to hide out permanently from life than it is to get mowed down by it. I've already submitted my application."

Graham's father snorted. "Some crazy kind of New Age business. You'll never make a go of it. There's no money in nonprofit businesses."

The Senior Partner looked disdainfully at him. "That's why they call them nonprofit. The Walnut Foundation isn't interested in making money. It's interested in helping people."

"Are you finished with us?" Graham's father asked. "Can we go now?"

"Not before you all sign some papers. Then you can go for good. Don't you want to know what's going to happen to your relatives who were inmates at Walnut Manor?"

"Oh, sure," Graham's father said. "What about them?"

"You'll be happy to know they've been examined by a team of doctors as to their mental and physical health, and the only one who could be considered to have any problems at all is Eddy. The others all fall well within the normal range on everything. Eddy's well physically, except for having no muscle tone from lying down for so long. Since he won't answer any questions, his mental state is hard to determine. But the Walnut Foundation will have doctors on its staff, specifically Dr. Waldemar, Dr. Malcolm, and Dr. Trinidad; and they'll see that he gets the best of care. Nice of you to be concerned."

"So everybody but Eddy will be coming home?" Virgil and Lyle's sister asked, aghast.

"Why would they want to do that?" the Senior Partner asked. "They're all going to stay on as staff at the Walnut Foundation. I expect they'll be drawing up new wills, too, now that they're of sound mind and body, leaving some of their relatives out."

There was a collective horrified intake of breath from the board of directors as the implications of that statement became clear to them.

"Where are the papers we have to sign?" Graham's father asked. "Let's get it over with."

part three

CHAPTER

21

- - - - - - -

Dr. Waldemar hurried across the brand-new parquet
floor of Walnut Manor to answer the brand-new front-
door bell. He would rather have been napping under an
umbrella out by the pool, but there was too much going
on today.

Standing on the brand-new front porch was Sid
Skeet in his yellow suit and pointed shoes to match.
With him was a young couple, the man well dressed
and pleasant looking, the woman pretty and pregnant.

"Hi, Sid," Dr. Waldemar said. "What can I do for
you?"

"Hi, Doc," Sid Skeet said. "This is Mr. and Mrs.
Blandings. They're thinking of buying that Federated
Conglomerates property on the other side of Walnut
Manor that's been for sale so long. But they'd heard
some . . . interesting things about Walnut Manor, so
they wanted to take a look before they decide for sure.
I promised them there's nothing to worry about, but
they wanted to see for themselves." He tapped the lapel

of Dr. Waldemar's tuxedo. "Kind of dressed up, aren't you?"

"We've got a wedding starting in a few minutes in the garden. Why don't you come out there with me? After the ceremony I'll show you around."

Sid Skeet and the Blandingses followed Dr. Waldemar through the sparkling downstairs of Walnut Manor, all freshly painted, with brass and glass newly polished. The dining room was set up for a buffet supper, dazzling with bright silver platters, tall arrangements of flowers, and zillions of white candles in crystal candelabras.

They went out through the dining-room doors into the garden, where wild roses climbed over an arbor, beneath which stood a clergyman in a long black robe and a white collar. Horatio sat in a gilded chair playing "Pennies from Heaven," Mr. Moreland's favorite song, on his guitar. Mousey accompanied him on her white piano, her filmy skirts spread out on the piano bench. Mr. Moreland, looking solemn and nervous and handsome in his black tuxedo and white beard, stood next to the clergyman. Lined up beside him, also dressed in tuxedos, were Captain Lester, Graham, Everett, Lyle and Virgil, Boom-Boom, Sandy, Bentley, Dr. Malcolm, and, propped up in an armchair looking like a doll with no stuffing, Eddy.

On the other side of the clergyman were Sunnie, Dr. Trinidad, and Flossie, all dressed in the same style of floaty gown Mousey was wearing, but each of a different pastel shade. They held old-fashioned bouquets of pink rosebuds and baby's breath, and all three had tears in their eyes. Louie and Attila, white bows around their necks, sat at the bridesmaids' feet, still and serious, as if they understood the importance of what was going on. Attila's feathers had finally grown back in, whiter and thicker than ever before.

Horatio and Mousey began Handel's "Wedding March," and out of the dining room doors came Opal. At least everyone assumed it was Opal. She looked a little bit like Opal. Her hair was curled, she had lipstick on, and white high-top basketball shoes with pearl trimmings. There were flowers in her curled hair and a sheaf of white roses in her arms, and her wedding dress was an intriguing combination of lace and sweatshirt fleece. There was no sign at all that she was chewing gum.

She winked at Dr. Waldemar and Sid Skeet, and the Blandingses, too, as she walked toward the arbor. Mr. Moreland, transfixed, watched her approach and began to smile. By the time she reached him and he took her hand, his smile stretched all the way across his face. Opal gave him a large self-possessed grin and lowered her eyes modestly to her roses.

Horatio and Mousey left their instruments and went to stand on either side of the arbor. Dr. Waldemar hurried to take his place, too.

The clergyman's stately and awesome words about sickness and health, richer and poorer, parting by death—which had special meaning for all those who had lived through the last year at Walnut Manor—twined around them the way the Christmas bubbles had, filling them with hope and wonder and love.

Captain Lester handed over Opal's ring, studded with large and glittering opals and diamonds, and Sunnie, diamond-bright tears on her smooth cheeks, handed over Mr. Moreland's. Then Mr. Moreland kissed Opal, a long and robust kiss, and the wedding was over. Opal the custodian and nurse had become Mrs. Whitney Hamilton Atherton Moreland III, wife of one of the richest men in the country, and she had gotten there merely by being her own crusty, stubborn, hardworking self.

In fact it was only that morning they had learned that Mr. Moreland was now considered one of the top *ten* richest men in the country. That was probably due to the fact that, for a wedding present, Captain Lester had paid him back all the money he owed him from their years of card games in the library at Walnut Manor. Captain Lester, who had made heaps of money from selling the manufacturing rights to his Investment game, was also in the top ten and hardly missed the amount he paid Mr. Moreland.

Mousey wiped her own tears on the hem of her floating gown and returned to her piano, where she struck up a lively recessional tune for the wedding party to hug each other to.

Mrs. Blandings dried the tears she found on her cheeks and said to her husband, "I've never been to a wedding where there were no guests and so many attendants."

"We were the guests, dear," he told her. "And I consider it an honor."

"Good thing we arrived when we did," Sid Skeet said. "It's a favorable omen, don't you think, for you to be the only guests at your new neighbors' wedding?"

Sid introduced everyone to the Blandingses as they filed into the dining room to begin the feasting. The Blandingses earned points with their neighbors-to-be by not commenting as Graham carried Eddy, in his armchair, into the dining room. And by agreeing with Everett, who shook their hands and said, " 'Take away love and our earth is a tomb.' Robert Browning. 1812 to 1889."

When the introductions had been made, Sid Skeet went over to the bride. "Hi, Opal. Or should I call you Mrs. Moreland?" he asked. "I must say, you could have knocked me over with a feather when I heard you were getting married. And to one of the inmates, too. Well, blow me down."

"I gather you got the rest of the story, too, Skeet," Opal said in her old familiar growl. "That there's nothing wrong with the inmates anymore—except for Eddy, of course—and that we're all working together now. So I'd appreciate it if you'd knock off your tired jokes about nuts and goofballs and wackos."

"Sure, sure," Sid said. "It's just still a little hard for me to believe. And all that stuff about the attempted murders. Are you *sure* that those things really happened?"

"Why don't you go visit Bart and Bernie in the slammer and ask them if it really happened? A jury found them guilty on every count. Of course they complained that it wasn't a jury of their peers."

Boom-Boom had come up beside them and was eavesdropping. At the mention of the trial, he couldn't restrain himself. "Oh, you should have seen them during the trial," he said. "We all went every day, after we finished testifying, just for the fun of watching them squirm and lie and try to weasel their way out of getting what they deserved. And when the verdicts came in, oh, it was wonderful!"

Everett, who had joined them, said, " 'Where law ends, tyranny begins.' William Pitt the Elder. 1708 to 1778."

"Well, there won't be any more tyranny from Bart and Bernie," Boom-Boom said. "The law took care of them. It makes me smile every time I think of them being hauled away in their jail overalls and chains, yelling about how they'd been framed and how it wasn't fair that they couldn't have Horatio's money after they'd tried so hard to get it and how they'd be good forever if Horatio would just pay them to be."

"It's not polite to gloat so much," Sunnie said, handing a glass of champagne to Boom-Boom. "And remember how sad it makes Horatio to know how eager his own brothers were to do him harm."

"Well, it makes me pretty sad to know what my

own mother wanted to do to me, too," Boom-Boom said.

"I know it does," Sunnie said. "But we should all be glad about our new lives."

"I am. But how come you don't look glad?" Boom-Boom asked her.

Tears welled in Sunnie's eyes. "Weddings always make me cry. Not because I'm sad, though. These are tears of happiness." The aforementioned tears began to slide down Sunnie's cheeks, and Boom-Boom was absolutely right: She didn't look glad at all, no matter what she said. She gave a shuddering little sob and pressed her handkerchief to her face. "Excuse me," she said, weeping. "I think I'll go upstairs for a while." And she ran out into the hall and up the wide front stairs.

Dr. Waldemar looked after her with concern as he led the Blandingses and Sid Skeet into the library to show them the list of classes that would be offered to the Walnut Foundation's first crop of frazzled escapees from the rat race. Those people would be arriving as soon as Mr. Moreland and Opal returned from their wedding trip to Switzerland. There are more banks per square foot in Switzerland than any place else in the world, and Mr. Moreland wanted to see them all. Opal was looking forward to two weeks of room service.

"The people you'll be seeing here at Walnut Manor," Dr. Waldemar said, "will look tired and distressed when they first arrive, but they should have the spring back in their steps, and the sparkle back in their eyes, when they leave. Each of us here on the staff has to leave periodically, too, so we can experience the outer world. Too much isolation makes us narrow and intolerant. In fact, Mousey Huntington-Ackerman will be leaving tomorrow to begin rehearsals as the star in a new stage play in the city. The director thinks she has the most beautiful voice he's ever heard. And Horatio and Sandy have just come back from conducting a financial seminar, where they were introduced as the most brilliant and financially creative father-and-son team in history. And Graham's been gone all summer to school in the city. We missed him a lot. We like it best when we can all be together, but we're learning that we can take one another with us in our hearts when we're away. Ah, here's the class list. If there's anything you'd like to sign up for, let us know. I'm sure we could fit you in."

On the wall beside the fireplace was a sign-up sheet for classes for the coming guests. Sunnie had planned them, since she had more ideas than anyone else did.

Mr. Blandings leaned forward and read:

"*Hello, Dali:* Introduction to Modern Art Appreciation
Everything You've Ever Wanted to Know about Sects: Introduction to Comparative Religions
Seoul Food: Introduction to Oriental Cooking
Feats of Clay: Introduction to Ceramics

Someday My Prints Will Come: Introduction to
    Photography
Some Like It Haute: Introduction to Fashion
    Design
Bag of Treks: Introduction to Travel Planning
First Come, First Serve: Tennis Lessons
Topographical Errors: Introduction to Geology"

"My goodness," Mrs. Blandings said, "they all sound just fascinating, though in my present condition," she patted her round tummy, "I think I'll have to pass up the tennis lessons."

"This is just the beginning," Dr. Waldemar said. "There'll be lots of other things going on, too. Virgil and Lyle are starting driving lessons, and Flossie's into gardening, and Bentley's the chemistry expert. You wouldn't know anyone in the market for an elixir that gives hiccups to chickens, would you?"

Sandy came into the library, looked around, and asked, "Has anybody seen Sunnie? It's time to cut the cake and we can't do it without everyone there."

"She went upstairs," Dr. Waldemar said. "Shall I go get her?"

"Please. And then you and Sid and the Blandingses must come into the dining room."

They were all gathered around the cake, Mr. Moreland and Opal holding the silver knife poised, when Dr.

Waldemar returned with Sunnie, red eyed and moist looking.

"Cut it, cut it!" Boom-Boom cried. And so they did, as Sunnie burst into a fresh torrent of tears.

During the long months of the spring and summer when all the residents of Walnut Manor and Eclipse had worked so hard to bring the Walnut Foundation into being, Sandy and Sunnie had labored side by side as colleagues and friends. But never again had their eyes met the way they had in the sickroom the day the sleepers wakened.

Sandy had tried, but Sunnie wouldn't cooperate, and he thought that once again, as he had during the Christmas kiss, he had read more into her response than was actually there. She had been surprised by his kiss, that's all. She had been thinking about something else as she gazed into his eyes; distracted, not dazzled as he was. The fact that she never wore his signet ring convinced him he had been foolish and forward to give it to her.

He had tried to resign himself to the ache in his heart every time he looked at her, but he wasn't doing well at it. The ache got achier. So now when he saw her sobbing over the wedding cake, he couldn't help himself: He went to her and put his arms around her.

"Please don't cry," he whispered into her small, seashell-shaped ear. "It breaks my heart to see you so unhappy. What can I do to cheer you up?"

"There's only one thing," she sobbed, soaking the

front of his tuxedo shirt with her tears, "and I could never ask you."

"What? I'll do anything." He held her tighter. He didn't care how soggy his shirt got. And they were both oblivious to the enthralled attention being paid them by everybody in the room.

"Then tell me exactly what's in your heart. I can't guess any longer."

"Oh, Sunnie, how can I do that? I don't want to offend you."

"What makes you think you would offend me?"

"I offended you on Christmas when I kissed you. I offended you when I gave you my signet ring. I offended you when I locked eyes with you the day Horatio and Mousey and Flossie and Attila woke up."

"Are you sure I was offended?" She drew back in his arms and looked up into his face. "Maybe I was just surprised and shy. Maybe I didn't know what you meant that ring to signify. I haven't had much experience with men, you know."

"Of course you have. You're young and beautiful and fascinating, and you've been out in the world while I've been shut up in a make-believe paradise turning into a world-class simpleton."

"But out in the world I never found anybody I felt about the way I feel about you. And I swore to myself I'd never kiss anybody until I could feel that way."

"What way?" Sandy asked, the ache in his heart changing to something else, something warm and expectant. "What way do you feel about me?"

"I can't tell you until I know how you feel about me."

"Can't you tell? Don't you know that I can sense when you've entered a room without even turning around and seeing you? Don't you know that you're in my dreams every night? Don't you know that you've brought a light into my life that I didn't even know existed? Why, Sunnie, I've loved you from the first day you came to Eclipse. How can you not know that?"

Sunnie's tears began to flow again, but this time the colors of the rainbow reflected from them, and her smile was so radiant, there seemed to be another light source in the room.

"And how can you not know," she said to Sandy, "that I've been afraid you were just being polite and friendly? That I've known I couldn't stay on at Walnut Manor if I found out polite and friendly is all you felt toward me. How can you not know that being wise and pure and gentle doesn't mean you're a simpleton? How can you not know that I've loved you from the first day I came to Eclipse?"

"Really?" he said, his face alight. "Would you wear my ring now if it was an engagement ring?"

She took his face in her hands and kissed him. And both of them were so lost in their new knowledge of each other that neither of them heard their friends, in a circle around them, clapping their hands and sniffling.

"Well, my goodness," Dr. Waldemar said. "Where was I when all this got started?"

"Isn't that sweet?" Flossie said, taking Bentley's arm and squeezing it.

"My baby," Mousey said, dabbing at her eyes with a white lace handkerchief as Horatio put an arm around her.

"I must say," he told her, "we men of Eclipse have excellent taste in women."

" 'The only abnormality is the incapacity to love.' Anaïs Nin," Everett said, and he rubbed the back of one hand surreptitiously across his eyes.

"Oooh, icky," Boom-Boom said in his little kid voice. "Why, not at all," he said in his grown-up voice. "It's rather touching."

Opal and Mr. Moreland didn't say anything because they were kissing each other, too.

Graham didn't even look at the wedding cake, unattended for the moment and perfectly situated for stealing. Instead, he was thinking about a red-haired girl he'd met at summer school.

"Perfectly natural biological response," Dr. Malcolm commented.

"It's somewhat more complicated than that," Dr. Trinidad said, a sentimental quiver in her melodic accent.

"You said it," Captain Lester added, giving Dr. Trinidad a closer appraisal. She looked like a million bucks' worth of double tax-free municipal bonds, he decided.

"Awwww," Virgil and Lyle said. "Just like on *The Love Boat*."

Sandy and Sunnie stopped kissing and gazed at each other. "Can we go to Hawaii on our honeymoon?" she asked. "I've been reading about volcanic islands lately."

"Why not?" Sandy said, gloriously happy. "We're going to sound like a Hawaiian weather report for the rest of our lives: sunny and sandy."

"You know, I'm suddenly feeling much better," Eddy said, struggling to sit up in his armchair.

And they all lived as happily ever after as real life will allow.